PIRATES
AND
PLUNDER

A division of Scholastic Ltd
London ~ New York ~ Toronto ~ Sydney ~ Auckland
Mexico City ~ New Delhi ~ Hong Kong

Published in the UK by Scholastic Ltd, 2010

Text copyright © Terry Deary, 2010
Illustrations © Martin Brown, 2010

ISBN 978 1407 10955 8

Printed and bound by Bookmarque Ltd, Croydon, Surrey

2 4 6 8 10 9 7 5 3

HORRIBLE HISTORIES

GORY STORIES

PIRATES AND PLUNDER

TERRY DEARY

ILLUSTRATED BY

MARTIN BROWN

SEAS AND SWABBIES

The Mediterranean Sea – Wednesday 1 August 1798

'**W**hen I was a pirate,' the one-eyed man said in a hoarse whisper, 'we sailed the seven seas!'

'What? *All* of them?' said a skinny boy with a skinny sneer on his skinny face.

The one-eyed man glared at him ... and it's hard to glare when you only have one eye. The skin of the man's face was like leather and his nose as curved as an eagle's beak. Wild grey hair sprouted from under his black hat and a golden earring hung from a dirty ear.

'Yes,' he hissed. '*All* of them. And we pirates had a way of dealing with cheeky young bed-bugs like you.'

The children and the women had been laughing at the pirate tales but now they went silent.

The ship creaked and strained as it was pushed through the sea by the hot south-westerly wind, a wind that had gusted over the dusty Sahara desert. Deep in the lower decks the crowd had gathered by the light of a mutton-fat lantern to hear the tales of terror.

The man leaned forward and pushed his curved nose close to the boy's. 'In the south seas there are mighty fish called sharks. They can scent a drop of blood ten miles away and swim towards it fast as lightning to a tall ship's mast.'

'I'm not frightened of fish!' the boy shrugged and tried to laugh but the laugh died in his throat.

'These *fish*,' the old man spat, 'can chop a man in half with one bite ... if the man is lucky.'

'That's *lucky*?' the boy squeaked.

'Oh, yes, that's a quick and sudden end. But if you're *un*lucky one shark takes your arm and another one takes your leg ... then another ... and you drown.'

'I can swim,' the boy boasted.

'Not without legs you can't,' the man said. 'They say there are sharks here in the Mediterranean ... off the coasts of Greece. So, young Jem Hawkwood, you put an anchor in that lip of yours or I'll take you there and throw you to the sharks.'

A large woman with arms as wide as a mizzen mast stood up. Her head touched the top of the low ceiling and her red hair blazed in the darkness. 'Don't you go threatening my son, Mad Mac,' she raged. 'You try to throw him to the fishes and you'll have to get past me.'

The man shook his head. 'Oh, I'll get past you, Meg Hawkwood. In fact I may slice off your ear and throw it in the water to bring the sharks ... then they'll be all ready to feast on your son. Sit down, woman.'

'You don't frighten me,' she muttered.

'Oh, yes I do,' he said quietly. Jem's ma sat down on the floor. No one looked at her. 'Where was I?' Mad Mac asked.

'Sailing the seven seas, when you were a pirate,' a small girl said.

Mad Mac nodded. 'I sailed with some of the most evil men ever to hoist a red flag!' he said. 'As you know, the *black* flag is the pirate signal for an enemy ship to lower her sails and stop. If they obey, we go on board and rob them ... if they *don't,* we raise the *red* flag, chase them and rob them anyway. But if they make us chase too hard – if they really annoy us – we throw them to the fishes.' The man's one eye rolled towards Jem as he said this.

'Tell us about William Fly!' a woman said. Her head was low as she sewed a shirt in the dim light.

'William Fly? As nasty a bit of ballast slime as you could wish to meet,' Mad Mac said. 'He started off sailing on a slave trader under Captain Green. But he led a mutiny of the men. They threw the captain over the side.'

'That's nasty,' the sewing woman agreed.

'Fly was fair! He gave the captain a choice! Jump or be thrown! Heh! Heh! Heh!' Mad Mac cackled.

'What happened to him?' the girl asked.

'Oh, the crew turned on him in the end – he used to have them lashed with whips for the smallest thing. Usually a hundred lashes. They handed him over to the Navy and the Navy hanged him,' Mad Mac sighed. 'But he had a good end!'

'He was *hanged,*' Meg Hawkwood gasped. 'How is that *good*?'

Mad Mac's eye glinted in the lantern light. 'William Fly stood on the gallows and gathered arms full of flowers the people threw at him. Then they came to put the rope around his neck and he stopped them. He said that whoever tied to noose had done a bad job ... so he tied it himself, slipped it over his neck and turned himself off! Her was mad as nest of wasps, was Will Fly, but I learned a lot from him. Pirating gave me a good life.'

Jem Hawkwood blew out his cheeks. 'If pirating is so good,' he said, 'How come you gave it up and joined the British Navy? You're here, fighting against the French – a plain seaman – why aren't you still pirating?'

Mac turned his eye on the boy. 'I said pirating *gave* me a good life. But it's not the same now ... no Spanish galleons full of gold, the slave trade is dying, and this war has ruined us; the rich French merchants never go to sea without French battleships to guard them. They're afraid of the British Navy. So here I am,' he scowled. 'But once the war is over ... oh, I'll be the greatest pirate since Blackbeard.'

'Tell us about Blackbeard!' one of the children cried.

'Ah!' the man cried. 'Me old mate Blackbeard! I'm one of the few men alive to tell the tale ... you see, Blackbeard used to shoot his own men for sport!'

The children gasped. 'That's what he did to his *friends*? What did he do his enemies?' the girl asked.

'He liked to steal rings – they were easy to sell back in port. But sometimes the rings were stuck on a prisoner's fingers. So Blackbeard told his men to just cut off a finger to get at the ring. And if the victim had lots of rings, and you didn't have much time, you should just cut off the whole hand. You could pull the rings off later.'

'Gruesome,' the girl shuddered.

'And he *looked* gruesome too.' Mad Mac twisted his fingers in his own scruffy beard and said, 'He wore his black beard in plaits so they looked like snakes. And when he went into battle he put lighted fuses in the plaits so his face was wrapped in smoke like a devil. And his strength was as great as a giant. If he chopped a man on the head with his cutlass the man would be split in half, clean to the waist!'

'But the British Navy got him in the end,' Jem Hawkwood argued.

'They did ... they sent Lieutenant Maynard to hunt him down. Maynard's ship, the *Pearl*, caught up with him and Blackbeard jumped on board. But Maynard was cunning ... he had most of his men below decks. Blackbeard hadn't seen them, of course. When Maynard gave the signal his sailors rushed up and attacked Blackbeard and the pirates. They shot Blackbeard ... but still he stood there – they shot him again ... and again. Then they began to chop at him with their cutlasses. Do you know it took *five* musket balls and twenty cuts to bring old Blackbeard down? Just to make sure he was dead, they lopped off his head and stuck it on the top of the mast!'

Oh, dear, there he goes again! Blackbeard died even earlier than William Fly. Blackbeard was hunted down and chopped up in 1718 – that is true. But Mad Mac wasn't there at the time. Why did the listeners not laugh at Mad Mac's stories? Because they never had a history lesson in their lives. They BELIEVED his bragging tales. Aren't you lucky you have me to keep you right?

'But what about his body?' one of the children cried.

'Tell us about the body!'

'They threw it over the side of the ship and it started to swim! The headless corpse swam three times around the *Pearl* before it sank.'

'And that was the end of Blackbeard?' the sewing woman asked.

'Perhaps! Before he set sail that last time, Blackbeard married Mary Ormonde ... a lovely lass in Portsmouth. She died of a broken heart when he didn't return. They say her ghost wanders the cliffs of England looking for his ship to come home. And one day, if you ask me, one day Blackbeard's ghost will go home to Mary.'

The ship rocked and swayed as it changed course and the timber sides groaned like Blackbeard's ghost.

10

Suddenly the door to the little room crashed open and let in the warm wind from the stairways above. A young man in a smart uniform with golden braid and buttons ducked in to the room. 'There you are Macdonald!' he said and his voice was as posh as paint. 'You idle, scurvy swabbie. Dodging the real work as usual. If I had my way I'd have you keel-hauled!'

Mad Mac's eye glared with a look of pure poison but he kept his voice soft. 'Lieutenant Darke, sir! How good of you to join us. For a moment I thought you were Admiral Nelson himself – looking so handsome in your shining shoes and your officer's hat. Oh, the ladies must love you, sir.'

The women giggled and Lieutenant Jacob Darke's hot face turned redder. It was a face with bulging eyes too large, a thin mouth and a weak chin that was just too small.

'The ladies are all married,' he said fiercely. 'But *you* have no place here, and *you*,' he said, pointing at Jem Hawkwood, 'you shouldn't be here either. You're not in the nursery. If I catch you idling down here again I'll have you lashed.'

'That's right,' Meg Hawkwood said. 'Pick on a little boy, why don't you?'

'He's a member of the crew,' Darke argued. 'He is paid. He is under Captain Foley the same as the rest of us. I'd have you women and children thrown off the fighting ships if I had my way. Thrown off!'

The women muttered angrily. The sewing woman said, 'We work hard ... I'm sewing a shirt for Captain Foley now.'

'And when we go into battle who is it that takes wine and water to the gunners to keep their strength up?' Meg Hawkwood demanded.

'The women!' the others cried.

'Then you'd better start gathering your wine and water cups now. Captain Foley has ordered us to take up battle stations now. Get moving! You, Macdonald,' he said, jabbing a finger at Mad Mac, 'help with clearing the decks for action.'

Mad Mac rose stiffly to his feet, 'No hurry, though, sir? I mean it's afternoon. The French are a few hours away. It'll be tomorrow morning before we're ready to fight. Nobody fights at night!'

Lieutenant Darke's eyes narrowed. 'Admiral Nelson fights in any way at any time he wants. Don't argue, just do as you're told.' He nodded towards Jem Hawkwood. 'And you get to the powder room now, monkey.'

The officer ducked out of the room and the others got ready to leave. Mad Mac's leathery lips turned down sourly. 'No one speaks to Mac like that. When the night is at its darkest – or the battle is at its fieriest – young

Lieutenant Darke may have a little accident. He won't be the first officer to vanish over the side of a ship – pirate ship or Navy ship.'

Mad Mac limped along the narrow passageway and up the stairs to the next deck. 'That's murder, Mac,' Jem said.

'That's not what my friend Blackbeard would call it. Remember Blackbeard was killed by a Navy Lieutenant, a fine and dandy young man just like Darke. Blackbeard wouldn't call it murder!'

'What would he call it?' the boy asked.

'He'd call it *revenge*,' the sailor said quietly. 'We may be on the same side right now – while we have the French to beat – but we won't always. He's been out to get me ever since we left England. No one calls me a swabbie and lives. No one.'

Jem Hawkwood shivered in the afternoon heat.

A swabbie is a lowly sailor who is only fit to swab (or wash) the deck. No one liked being called a swabbie – even if they were one! You understand? I mean, you wouldn't like being called a half-brained, pudding-headed prawn ... even though you are one, would you?

MONKEYS AND MACHINES

Lieutenant Darke felt the dry breeze on his face as he reached the deck. The sun was slipping down the cloudless sky to the west but the desert wind still burned like the breath of a cannon.

The crew of *Goliath* swarmed over the decks, wrapping ropes, stowing sails, running up rigging, swinging on spars, coiling cordage, hauling halyards, bundling buntlines, grabbing for gunters, battling with baggywrinkles and battening hatches ready for battle.

Of course you don't need me to tell you what that all means, do you? Good. If you don't know your buntlines from your baggywrinkles you'll have to IMAGINE the scene. Thank you.

The men worked quickly and the Lieutenant felt their joy of finally going into the fight. But he didn't share their excitement. He was still raging with hatred for Seaman Macdonald. As he walked toward the stern of the ship he muttered, 'In a battle sailors go missing. When it's dark and cannonballs are flying, he wouldn't be the first sailor to vanish over the side of the ship.' He gripped the hilt of the sword that hung from his waist till his knuckles turned white.

Lieutenant Darke climbed to the poop deck, the high

deck at the back of the ship, and looked back. The British fleet of fifteen ships stretched back in a line that disappeared over the horizon. *Goliath* was in the lead by half a length from the *Zealous* and Darke smiled at last. Captain Hood on the *Zealous* wouldn't like to be beaten into the battle by *Goliath*. Darke raised his hat and waved to the crew of *Zealous*.

'Ah, there you are, Mister Darke,' Captain Foley said. The captain was not much older than Darke but his calm face looked strong and no one argued with his soft voice. 'Come into the cabin at once,' he said and led the way in. 'We'll reach the French in an hour's time. A scout has dropped off this plan,' he said, pointing to a parchment on the table. The officers gathered closer to look.

They didn't need to be told the map showed the north coast of Egypt. Napoleon Bonaparte had landed an army there. The British Navy wanted to sink his ships – trap the fighting Frenchman so Napoleon couldn't leave.

In the shade of the captain's cabin it was a little cooler. Daylight sparkled through the small windows and showed the ship's officers crowded into the little space.

'Here are our friends the French,' Captain Foley said and tapped the plan.

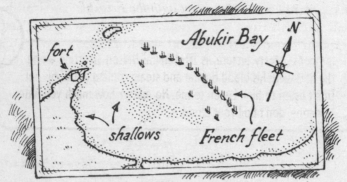

'There they are, gentlemen, in line of battle, anchored, waiting for us. They are mostly chained to each other in that line so we can't sail through them. They have all their guns pointing out to sea. As soon as we sail alongside they will try to blow us out of the water.'

'But we'll be trying to blow them out of the water at the same time,' Master Gunner White said. He was a grey-bearded man with scarred hands and a face with more creases than an old canvas sail.

'We *could* do that,' Captain Foley nodded. 'We'd lose a lot of lives, a few ships and probably lose the battle.'

'Oh, but I say! We have to try, sir. It's better to die trying!' Lieutenant Darke cried.

'Remember what our Admiral Nelson says?'

'He says lots of things,' the master gunner told him. 'He says we must hate the French like we hate the devil!'

Lieutenant Darke nodded and raised his small chin as if he were Nelson himself. 'He said, *My blood boils at the name of a Frenchman! Down, down with the French!*'

It's not a pretty picture, is it? Admiral Nelson strutting along the deck with his blood boiling and steam coming out of his hat. Don't listen to him. Listen to me. No matter how much you hate someone, don't boil your blood.

Captain Foley smiled. 'He also said we have to look for any advantage we can. Look at their ships. Where can we get an advantage?'

The officers shook their heads. The captain ran his finger on a line to the left of the French ships. 'What if we sail between their ships and the shore? That's the sort of thing Nelson would ask.'

The others gasped. 'We'd run aground on the sand!' someone said.

'We captured a French ship last week. Our ship *Culloden* is towing her along now. On that ship we found these French maps here. The French have done charts of just how deep the water is. They show there is just enough water between the French and the beach for us to squeeze through.'

'It's a bit of a risk, sir' Lieutenant Darke muttered.

'And Admiral Nelson says *nothing* is sure in a sea fight – there are risks whatever we do.'

Master Gunner White was excited. 'They will have all

their guns facing the other way! We'll hit them before they can turn their guns around! It's worth the risk!'

'It's a bit like stabbing a chap in the back,' Lieutenant Darke muttered. 'Not very sporting, I say.'

'Either that or let *him* stab *us* in the front!' the captain laughed.

The others agreed. Captain Foley filled cups with wine and passed them around his officers. 'Gentlemen, a toast. Good health to Admiral Nelson ... and the devil take the French!'

The officers drank and gave a cheer. Then they hurried to their jobs – to steer the ship, to load the guns, to raise the right sails and to tell the men of the plan.

It was six o'clock. They would reach the French line in an hour.

***

The powder room was deep down at the bottom of the ship where no enemy cannon shot could set it on fire. 'One spark and the whole ship is blown into splinters,' Meg Hawkwood had told her son. 'You don't carry a candle or any sort of light in there. There is a candle burning outside the window and you work by the light of that.'

Jem Hawkwood stepped inside the powder room now and trembled. He used a wooden shovel to scoop the gunpowder from the wooden hold ... no iron to make a spark. He filled bags, ready to carry them up to the gunners.

'When the battle
starts, you bring up
the powder as fast as
your legs will carry you,'
the master gunner had told
the boys – the powder monkeys.
'We can't have too much on deck
before the battle. Why not?'

'Please, sir, because if it catches fire the whole ship
would explode or the sails and the rigging would catch
fire,' Jem had said.

Master Gunner White had nodded. 'Good lad.'

Jem had felt pleased.

'And if we don't get enough powder up to the gun
decks?'

'The guns will stop firing and the enemy can sink us,' a
girl had said. She wasn't supposed to be a powder monkey
but no one would stop her if she wanted the job.

'The trick is to have just the right amount of powder
to the gunners at just the right time.'

And for weeks they'd practised. They sailed eastwards
across the Mediterranean Sea and ran up and down from
the powder room to the gun decks till they knew the way
with their eyes closed.

'Aha!' You cry. 'That's daft! They wouldn't be doing it with their eyes closed so why bother?' 'Oho,' I cry back. 'But in the smoke and fog of battle they would be almost as blind.' You didn't think of that, did you?

It was warm and dry down there and smelled of tar and sulphur. Jem made some bags of powder ready then went up through the decks to find his mother.

She was filling leather bottles with fresh water and wine. 'What's it like in a battle, Ma?' the boy asked.

The woman shrugged her broad shoulders. 'Noisy,' she snorted.

'Scary?' he asked.

She swept her long, red hair back and tied it tightly in a dark blue ribbon. 'Not at the time,' she said. 'You don't have time to think. You get your head down and do your job. If you're up on deck when a cannonball lands or a mast falls then you could be killed, I suppose. But if you hide down in the bilges you could be drowned if a hole is punched in the side.' She looked at him and held his shoulders. 'On a battleship – a ship of the line – there's no place to hide ... so there's no point trying.'

'Are the French really devils like Nelson says?' he asked.

She laughed. 'No, son. In my last battle we sank a French ship. Some of her sailors swam across to us and we hauled them up through our gun ports. They were poor helpless sailors just like ours ... with pompous, stuffed-up officers...'

'Just like ours?' Jem grinned.

'Just the same.'

Jem started filling bottles and thought for a while. 'So, Ma? If they're not devils, and they're just like us ... why are we fighting them?

'Because of the Revolution, son. You've heard us talk about it, haven't you?'

'Yes, Ma, but what's the Revolution?'

Meg Hawkwood stretched and sat on a chest. 'About ten years ago the French peasants were starving. Your dad landed there once – before the war – and he said most of the ploughmen and their wives had no shoes or stockings. The children looked hungry. Their clothes were so ragged they may as well not have had any. He saw one little girl whose only toy was a stick. He said it made his heart ache to see her.'

An English writer, Tobias Smollett, said those peasants were 'more like starved scarecrows than human beings'. I wonder why they didn't just get jobs as scarecrows then? You just stand around in a field all day with your shirt stuffed with itchy straw while birds peck at your head? Maybe not.

The peasants saw all the rich folk eating well and they were jealous. They decided it was time to kill the lot of them – the lords, the landowners, the bishops ... even the king and queen.'

Jem gasped. 'How did they do it?'

'They invented a machine to kill people. Now, they may not be devils but I tell you, that machine was the work of a devil. A doctor called Guillotin made a machine that chops off heads as quick as wink. You put the neck on a block, pull out a pin, and a great heavy blade drops down. Remember the factory you worked in back in England?'

'Yes, Ma.'

'Well you know how the great machines turned out cloth, day and night, non-stop? Cotton in one end, material out the other?'

'Yes, Ma.'

'Well the Revolution was a bit like that ... the lords and ladies in one end ... heads and bodies out the other. Thousands of them!'

'Even the queen?' Jem asked.

'*Especially* the queen – she was called Queen Marie Antoinette. She tried to run away from the mob. Your dad read a newspaper once that told the story of what the peasant women screamed when the queen was caught!' Meg Hawkwood climbed on the chest and acted out the French fury. 'Cut her throat and tear her skin for hair-ribbons. Wring her neck – tear her heart out. Fry her liver. I'll eat her legs. I'll have her guts. And I'll have her kidneys cooked in wine.'

'And they sent her to the chopping machine?'

'The guillotine, they call it. Yes, she went there a few years ago.'

'So who is king?'

'No one! A group of people rule the country. And the top man is this soldier they call Napoleon Bonaparte – a vicious little man if ever there was one. He won't be satisfied till he's come across the sea to kill our old King

George. He won't be happy till France rules the world. Make us all his slaves. That's why we're fighting them. That's why your dad died fighting him.'

'Will he win?' Jem trembled. 'In the end? Will Napoleon win?'

'Napoleon may win a few battles on land with his army ... but he will never, ever beat the British Navy at sea, Jem. Never. Napoleon rules the land – Admiral Nelson rules the waves ... so long as there are brave lads like you to fight of course.

Some of the women were gathering in the galley and heard them talking. 'That's the spirit, Meg.'

One of the women began to sing. Soon the others joined in. As the song spread out onto the decks the sailors picked it up. From the top of the mast to the lowest gun deck the voices rang out. Sailors on the *Zealous* added their voices across the warm breeze till it seemed as if the sea itself was singing...

'Rule, Britannia!
Britannia, rule the waves,
Britons never, never, never shall be slaves.'

As the last words died, a single voice cried from high above them, at the top of the main mast. 'Enemy sighted! French fleet three leagues ahead!'

'You're not afraid are you, Jem?'

Jem straightened his back. ''Course not, Ma. 'Course not!'

Meg Hawkwood slapped her hands together. 'Here we go!'

23

PLOTS AND POWDER

Jem Hawkwood spilled powder on the deck. He bent to scoop it up before the captain saw it. As he did he heard voices coming from behind a bundle of sails.

Some of the crew were in a cramped den where no one could see them, hoping to dodge the worst of the work. Jem knew who they were.

The boy knew they were the only four sailors on the *Goliath* who hadn't joined in with the singing. They had been hauling on ropes with faces as sour as unripe lemons. They worked when the officers were watching ... they idled when they weren't.

While the other sailors ran around the decks and up the rigging, the bitter-faced four slouched and dragged their bootless feet. Now they had slipped into a hiding place.

They were Grundle and Hope, Isaac and Jones.

Grundle and Hope, Isaac and Jones had been at sea for two months. Two months too long in their minds.

'What are we doing here?' Isaac said. He had a pointed face, like a weasel.

Great-gutted Grundle sighed. 'You know that.'

'You know that!' weedy Jones echoed like a parrot.

'It was the press gang!' the pasty-faced Hope reminded him.

'It was the press gang,' Jones moaned.

'How could we be so stupid?' Isaac sighed.

'You know that,' Grundle grumbled.

'You know that,' Jones groaned.

'We were sitting in *The Jolly Sailor* tavern,' Hope went on.

'Hah! That's a name, I say that's a name. *Jolly* sailor?' Grundle said with a harsh laugh. 'I'm not a jolly sailor.

'I'm not a jolly sailor neither,' Jones nodded.

'But we're all sailors!' Hope argued.

Grundle shook his large head and mumbled to himself, 'No. We are traders on little ships that never leave sight of the coast – we carry coal and vegetables, cloth and iron...'

'I'm a fisherman,' Isaac put in.

'Yes and we can still smell it on you, Isaac. Do you never wash your shirt?' Grundle argued.

Isaac sniffed. 'I can't smell anything wrong with me.'

'It was the *Jolly Sailor* that did for us though,' Jones said.

'We were having a peaceful drink,' Grundle said.

'Not *that* peaceful. I think we were arguing about whose turn it was to pay,' Hope reminded him.

'We were having a *fairly* peaceful drink. Then that feller walked in with a jar of rum,' Grundle went on.

'He *said* he'd pinched it from a Navy ship. He *said* we could all help him get rid of it,' Isaac nodded.

'He said he couldn't drink it all himself, so would we *help* him,' Hope remembered.

'Of course we were being friendly ... helpful ... doing a sailor a favour!' Grundle cried. 'And what happened?'

'We emptied the whole jar between us,' Jones said.

'Every last drop,' Grundle nodded.

Jones ranted. 'Then he told us where we could get *more* – he knew where the Navy rum store was with an open door – he said we could have a jar *each* if we wanted.'

'We were greedy,' Hope sighed.

'So he led us down those dark alleys till we were lost – I thought I knew Portsmouth harbour, but I'd never been down those lanes,' Isaac shivered.

'Then those bullies jumped on us,' Jones said. 'The press gang. Hit me over the head. I woke up on this tub.'

'It's not right,' Grundle spat.

'It's wrong,' Jones said.

Of course Jones was WRONG. The law said it was FINE for the Navy to grab men from the ports and force them to join the Navy. Hundreds were snatched, especially when there was a war on. Imagine YOU are walking down the street tomorrow and someone snaffles you. 'Sorry, mate,' they say. 'But we need someone to fly a new rocket ship to Mars.' You'd be upset – you'd understand how Grundle and Hope, Isaac and Jones felt.

'And NOW,' Jones whined, 'we're going into battle! We'll be shot at with cannons and muskets. You don't get that on a fishing boat.'

'I once had a nasty nip from a crab,' Hope told him.

'The crab didn't have a twenty-pound cannonball in its claws,' Jones said sourly. 'If we get through this battle I'm getting off this ship.'

Grundle shook his head. 'Jones, we are on the edge of the Sahara desert. What's the point of jumping ship here? There are tribesmen out there that will cut off your nose if they catch you.'

'And cut off your ears!' Isaac added.

'I've heard they will even cut off bits that are so disgusting I can't even tell you!' Grundle hissed.

This is horrible history ... but true. The French soldiers who landed with Napoleon were terrified of being lost in the desert. They thought that the tribes would cut off their bits and probably end up by cutting off their heads. Mind you, Napoleon had 900 Egyptian rebels beheaded and he had the heads rolled out on the street in front of the Egyptians as a lesson. Still, I have to say, Grundle was right ... jumping ship in Egypt in 1798 was NOT a clever plan. As clever a plan as you jumping a block of flats.

'We have to do something,' Isaac said fiercely.

Grundle lowered his head. 'There's a swabbie on this ship with one eye ... Mad Mac. He was pressed, just like us. He knows a lot about pirate ways. He told me he has a plan to get off the *Goliath* AND make a fortune. But he needs the help of a few trusty lads.'

'Us?' Isaac asked.

'Us,' Jones said.

'What's the plan?' Hope wondered.

'I don't know ... but it sounds like a good idea to me. All we have to do is live through this battle,' Grundle said.

Suddenly a sunset shadow fell over Grundle and Hope, Isaac and Jones. They looked up and found Lieutenant Darke standing over them. 'Get back to work, you idle scum,' he said and drew his sword. He used the flat of the blade to slap each man on the arms and chest till they scampered out of the cosy nook between the sails and on to the deck. 'Get bags of sand ready. When the battle starts you will scatter the sand in the pools of blood so the rest of us don't slip on the deck. Understand?'

'I hope Mad Mac's plan includes Lieutenant Darke ending up in a pool of blood,' Grundle murmured as he hurried off to do his duty.

Jem Hawkwood ran from the place where he'd been spying and carried on taking powder to the gunners.

'French navy one league away!' the lookout called.

***

Captain Foley stood at the rail on the poop deck and grinned as the French ships loomed larger. 'We'll be the first into the battle,' he called to the crew and they replied with a cheer. 'The Frenchies are expecting us to sail down their starboard side ... that's where all their cannon will be loaded and ready. But we are going to sail down their larboard side and blast them with our *larboard* cannon.'

Sailors use strange words like 'poop deck'. They also say 'starboard' when they mean 'right' and 'port' when they mean 'left'. But in the days of Napoleon's wars they called the left side 'larboard'. All starboard? Good. Concentrate or you'll be larboard behind.

The crew laughed. At the last moment the captain gave the order to steer to the larboard side of the French line. As *Goliath* drifted like a ghost past the first French ship, Jem lingered long enough to see that the French gun ports weren't even open. As they passed the second ship in the line it was the same and Captain Foley gave the order to drop anchor.

Jem raced down the steps to the powder room where women and children were calmly filling powder bags.

The whole ship shook as the larboard cannon fired at the same time. Jem had felt this a dozen times in training runs but in battle it thrilled him.

When he reached the deck Meg Hawkwood said, 'Powder to the starboard guns, my lad!'

'Why?' Jem asked.

His mother grabbed him by the front of his shirt and her powerful arms lifted him off his feet. 'In a battle you NEVER waste time arguing with orders. Just do it!' she said fiercely.

'Yes, Ma!' he squeaked. He ran to the starboard gun decks with his powder and looked through the port. A small French warship was heading towards them.

'It's a frigate,' the gunner said. 'Frigates don't usually get mixed up in battles between ships of the line. They're too small.'

'But they have guns! They can still shoot at us!' Jem trembled.

The gunner snorted. 'They can fire three hundred pounds of shot at us ... they might scratch us. But we'll be firing eight hundred pounds back. Who do you think is going to win this little battle, eh?'

Jem nodded. The master gunner appeared at the end of the gun deck. 'Load the cannon with double shot, the captain says! It's a frigate called the *Serieuse*.'

The men cheered and went about their task as Jem ran back to the powder room to get more gunpowder. The roar from the starboard cannon seemed enough to shake *Goliath* apart. Jem ran on to the deck to see the results. The *Serieuse* had lost all her masts and was slowly beginning to slide down into the sunset sea.

This was the battle between the French frigate Serieuse and Goliath. Forget the Bible story where little David licked giant Goliath. In a sea battle 1500 pounds of cannon shot will smash 300 pounds. In this true story, big Goliath swatted little Serieuse aside with a single blow.

French sailors – the ones that were still alive - flapped in the water like fish in a net and the *Goliath* crew threw ropes down to help haul them aboard. Injured French men and boys collapsed on the decks, defeated and dumb.

'Back to the larboard side,' Mrs Hawkwood said as she passed Jem on the stairways. He didn't argue. He ran past Mad Mac who was leaning on a rail, watching.

'Why don't the French turn around?' Jem asked. 'If their starboard guns are ready to fire?'

'Because they are all chained together,' Mac said.

'I forgot,' Jem said.

'Then it's just as well you're not our captain,' the man told him. 'This is not the way to fight,' he sighed. 'When I was a pirate we didn't blast away at each other with guns! We ran alongside the enemy, climbed aboard and fought them hand to hand with knives and swords and pistols!'

'What does it matter so long as we win?' Jem asked.

The pirate turned his eye towards the boy. 'It's a waste of good ships, lad. If we capture a ship with hardly any damage, it's one more ship for us and one less for the enemy. Now, a man like me could have done things with a ship like that,' he said as he watched the shattered French frigate slipping below the darkening waves.

'Done what, Mr Macdonald?'

'Made our fortune, lad. Made our fortune.'

PUNCH AND DUTY

The French fought back. At last they reached their larboard gun ports and their powder monkeys found the gunners.

Jem Hawkwood had felt the blast of the guns from *Goliath* but he had never felt the blows of enemy cannonballs hitting her.

There was shuddering and shivering, smashing and smoke, splinters and slivers of spars and quivering of decks, cries and screams and above all, streams of blood from shot and shattered crew. In the savage slaughterhouse the gunners' gore ran across the floor.

> The middle gun deck was the most dangerous place to be as it got the greatest battering. The sailors called it 'the slaughterhouse'. You can picture it, can't you? Unless you are having your tea as you read this.

Mad Mac the pirate swabbed the decks – so the blood wouldn't sicken the sailors – and Grundle and Hope, Isaac and Jones scattered sand over the slippery patches. The women helped the wounded away to the calm lower decks to bandage the wounds and stop their bleeding, to give water and wine and sometimes just to comfort with a quiet hand.

On his third trip to the larboard guns Jem heard the gunners give a mighty cheer ... another British ship was joining them in the line. The crew of *Theseus* cheered back and dropped anchor so her guns were facing the French ship *Le Peuple Souverain*. The French crew tried to reply with a cheer but it was weak. The crew of *Goliath* laughed.

There was a quiet pause in the firing and Captain Foley cried to the crew, 'Bring down the mast and flag of *Le Peuple Souverain*!'

The captain was the only man out in the open ... captains did brave things like that. Cannonballs flew around him and snapped ropes lashed at his legs but he stood firm with his hand on his sword.

The mast of *Le Peuple Souverain* was finally smashed, but a French sailor was sent up the rigging to nail the flag back onto the stump. 'Keep firing!' Captain Foley called and the guns pounded out their drumbeat of deadly iron.

The sky was dark but the flashes of cannon and a rising moon showed that half of the British fleet had sailed down the starboard side of the French line. Now the French ships were under fire from both sides.

Jem shook his head. The powder monkeys on the French ships wouldn't know which side to run to next. Then the sky began to lighten. One of the French ships had caught fire.

The deck hands, Mad Mac, Grundle and Hope, Isaac and Jones stopped to watch. Fire was the greatest fear of the crews. Gunshot would shatter, but fire would burn right down to the powder room and even the mightiest ship would be blown up like a bomb of wood and canvas, iron and flesh.

'The *Orient* is on fire,' Captain Foley cried. 'Stand ready with water buckets in case some of her lands on us!'

Grundle and Hope, Isaac and Jones moved to lower buckets over the side of the ship and gather seawater.

Jem stopped to watch as the fire spread on the French ship. Flames rippled up the masts to the top. In the dazzling glare he saw Frenchmen jump into the water clutching at wreckage and kicking their weary legs as fast as they could. The ones who reached *Goliath* were pulled aboard and left gasping on the decks.

Suddenly Jem felt a mighty blow across his shoulders. He was flung forward onto the deck and he threw out his arms to break his fall. A pain shot through his wrists and he cried out. He rolled over to see Lieutenant Darke standing over him. 'What are you doing, boy?' the officer shouted. The flames of the French ship shone red-orange in his eyes. He'd struck Jem with the flat of his sword and now the sword pointed at the powder monkey's chest. 'We are in a battle! You don't stand and watch, you idle, scurvy, son-of-a-rat. You *work*!'

Lieutenant Darke swung his sword at Jem's shoulder but the boy managed to roll out of the way.

Jem struck the side of the ship and there was no place left to go. He closed his eyes as Darke looked as if he was going to strike again. 'Lieutenant Darke!' Captain Foley's voice rang out.

Jem slowly opened his eyes. The captain was walking down the larboard steps of the poop deck and onto the main deck. 'Yes, sir?' the lieutenant asked and walked over to the captain, who stood in the shelter of the poop deck.

'Give the order to cease firing and raise some sail to get us away from the *Orient* before she explodes.'

The captain disappeared into his cabin and the lieutenant began barking orders. 'Grundle and Hope, Isaac and Jones ... man the sails and raise the jibs.'

The four press-ganged men slouched off to the bows to obey. Mad Mac loomed over Jem, reached down and gripped him by the elbows. He pulled the boy to his feet. 'I saw that, lad. It's time we had our revenge on

Lieutenant Darke, don't you think?'

'What are you going to do?' the boy asked.

'The officer is going to be hit by a cannonball! These things happen in battle,' he said with a sour smile and disappeared into the shadows on the starboard side.

'What's wrong?' Meg asked, coming up from the lower decks. 'Why have we stopped firing?'

Jem nodded his head towards the blazing *Orient*. The woman nodded, then looked at her son in the orange and blue light of flames and moon. 'Are you injured, son?'

He shook his head. 'No ... just Lieutenant Darke gave me a beating for standing idle.'

'He did, did he?' Mrs Hawkwood growled. Her face was as red as her bloodstained hands.

'Hurry up, Grundle and Hope, Isaac and Jones – we haven't got all night!' the officer cried from where he stood on the main deck.

Mrs Hawkwood strode across to him. Jem saw what happened next as if it were happening slower than treacle dripping off a spoon – though really it was over in moments.

Meg Hawkwood stood in front of Lieutenant Darke and rolled up her sleeves. 'You hit my son!' she said.

'I punished an idle urchin,' the officer sneered.

In the amber light of the burning French ship Jem saw a movement up on the poop deck behind the officer. Mad Mac had picked up a cannonball and was walking towards the rail.

'The lad has run up and down stairs for two hours without a rest,' Mrs Hawkwood argued.

'In a battle everyone works without a rest, woman!'

Mac stretched out his arms so the cannonball was held over Lieutenant Darke's head.

'Don't call me *woman*!' Mrs Hawkwood exploded.

'Look out!' Jem cried.

Mrs Hawkwood glanced up and saw Mac. He was about to let go of the cannonball.

Mrs Hawkwood let fly with a fierce punch.

She struck Lieutenant Darke on the chin and lifted him and his polished shoes off the deck. He flew backwards and struck the cabin wall. He may have made a cracking sound as his head hit the wall but no one heard. At the same instant, Mac's cannonball struck the deck.

Mrs Hawkwood looked up as the would-be cannonball-killer slid away.

At that moment the night was lit by a light as pure as white gold. Moments later the air shook with the sound of the explosion. Then the whole of *Goliath* was hit by a wind far fiercer than the Sahara's breeze.

It was a sparking hot hurricane that left glowing cinders in the tarred ropes and rigging, in the mighty masts and over the bound sails. The captain tore open the door to his cabin. 'All hands on deck, Lieutenant Darke...' he looked down at his feet and saw the lieutenant lying on the deck. The captain glanced at Meg Hawkwood. 'What happened?'

She shrugged. 'He'll be all right.'

Captain Foley looked across to Jem. 'You, monkey ... get all the crew on deck to wash away the sparks before we join the *Orient* at the bottom of the sea. Move!'

It took half an hour before *Goliath* was safe again. The weary crew slumped on the decks. It was 3 a.m. The night was turning quiet now. The crew of *Goliath* would get a little rest before morning brought more fighting.

Still the French fought on, all the next day and through the next night. A few French ships had slipped away into the dark sea – the British were too tired and damaged to chase them – but one by one the rest were smashed to ruin. One by one they lowered their flags.

Everyone knew how it would end.

***

Abukir Bay – Friday 3 August 1798

The sun rose in a smoky sky and showed the broken wreckage of a mighty French fleet. The water was scum-stained and scattered with broken bodies. Small boats rowed from ship to ship with messages.

When the men were rested and the women had given them a breakfast of bread and watered rum, Captain Foley stood up on the poop deck and gathered the crew below him. 'It is a victory to us,' he said. The men managed a weak cheer. 'Napoleon is trapped in Egypt and Britain is saved ... thanks to you.'

'How is Admiral Nelson?' a gunner called. 'Someone said he was hit.'

'He was blown down by a French shot. It tore a flap of skin off his forehead and the skin fell over his eye. As you know he only has one eye ... the flap of skin closed his good eye so he was blinded.'

Some of the crew chuckled. 'He wouldn't like that.'

'He sent a message to his wife,' Captain Foley said with a small smile. '*Tell her goodbye and say that I loved her!*'

'Did he die?' the gunner asked.

'No, he's been patched up.'

For the first time in hours the men's laughter rippled over the warm waves.

Patched up ... Geddit? Do you have friends like that? They scratch their knee in a football game and want you to call an ambulance. Nelson was a bit like that ... one of Britain's great heroes ... but always sure every wound would be his last. Of course one wound WAS his last: the last one.

'We have thirty-two men injured and one officer,' Captain Foley said. His face grew serious now. 'Lieutenant

Darke was knocked out. He is now awake and he is saying it wasn't a French gun that hit him.'

Grundle and Hope, Isaac and Jones looked at one another. Mad Mac's mouth was a hard, thin line. Jem Hawkwood's mouth went dry. His mother raised her chin and let the warm breeze lift her red hair. They all knew what was coming.

Captain Foley lowered his head for a few moments then lifted it and let his gaze sweep over the crew. 'Men fight on board ship. It happens. I may throw a violent man into chains for a few days till he cools off. Men who fight each other in the middle of a battle are bigger fools, but I have seen it happen. They will be given fifty lashes before they are thrown into the darkest, most stinking hold on this ship.'

And still the crew waited.

'But striking an *officer* ... at *any* time ... in battle or on shore, at sea or at a tavern in port...' He took a deep breath. 'The first duty of any man on a ship is to obey an officer. Your *duty*. There is only one punishment for a man who strikes an officer. If he is found guilty he will be brought on deck. He will have a rope placed around his neck and he will be hanged from the topmost mast so all the fleet can see.'

'That's not fair!' Jem cried. 'It's not like murder!'

'It is,' the captain said. 'We are in King George's Navy. We are not a bunch of pirates. Striking an officer is the worst crime any person on this ship can commit. The criminal will be hanged. They *will*.'

'I did it,' Jem said in a clear voice. 'He hit me with his

sword. I picked up a block and tackle and swung it at him.'

The captain shook his head. 'Lieutenant Darke is quite clear. It was a woman who hit him. A large woman with red hair.'

'That'll be me, then,' Meg Hawkwood said, stepping forward and wrapping a heavy arm around her son's shoulders.

Captain Foley sighed. 'Take her below decks,' he said to one of his officers. 'Keep her in chains. We'll put her on trial this evening when we've cleared up after the battle. She can hang tomorrow morning.'

Meg Hawkwood marched towards the officer and let him tie her wrists. Jem ran to Mad Mac. 'She hit him to save his life,' the boy hissed. 'Your life too. She hit him to knock him out of the way of *your* cannonball.'

The pirate spread his hands. 'So?'

'So ... you should do something to save her!'

'And I will, Jem lad. I will,' Mad Mac promised.

TALES AND TRIALS

Jem Hawkwood picked his way through the sick and wounded men who lay in the hold of the ship. Some of the wounds, even in the dim lantern light, were too horrible to look at. But the women washed them and bandaged them without complaining.

The smell was sickening in the hot and airless room.

There was a screen made from an old sail in one corner. Jem heard a weak voice from behind the screen saying, 'If you have to cut the arm off then do it quickly, Doctor.'

The ship's doctor replied, 'Give him a large glass of rum then hold him down.' There was a clinking as the doctor sorted through his saws and knives.

Jem hurried through the low door into the next hold where his mother sat on the floor, ankles and wrists chained. A woman was feeding her tea and hard ship's biscuits. Meg Hawkwood spat out a beetle from the biscuit she was chewing and smiled at the boy. 'My son, Jeremiah, come to visit his old mother. How are you, son?'

Jem choked and swallowed tears. 'All right, Ma. You?'

The woman chuckled. 'Oh, I'm fine for now, son. Ask me again tomorrow morning and I'll be even better!'

'Will you?'

'Yes! I'll be singing with the angels!' she laughed.

'Oh, Ma!' Jem cried. 'It's not funny. You shouldn't be making a joke of it.'

She shrugged her large shoulders. 'You want me to spend my last hours on earth being miserable?'

'No ... but ... but what'll I do without you?'

'You have a job here in the crew, lad. In time you'll become a gunner. You'll travel the world the way your Pa and I did. I've crossed the Atlantic Ocean to fight the Americans. I've been to the south and seen little fish that will tear your flesh off in seconds and leave you a skeleton ... piranhas they call them. I've seen jungles with parrots flying like rainbows ... and rainbows, after a storm, that look like chests of jewels. Oh, you have a good life ahead of you, Jem. Better than being stuck serving ale in some filthy tavern ... like I used to. Or working the knitting machines in a noisy factory ... like you used to.'

'I'll be an orphan, Ma,' Jem moaned.

'We're all orphans if we live long enough,' she smiled. 'Did I ever tell you the tale of Rachel Wall?'

'No, Ma,' Jem said. He loved to hear his mother's tales.

She took a sup of tea and began. 'Rachel lived on the other side of the Atlantic. She was just 16 years old when she took a trip to a place called Pennsylvania.'

'In America, Ma?'

'In America, Jem. She met a fisherman called George Wall at the docks and went off and married him. Just like that. Together they came up with a great plot to rob the rich folk up in Boston.'

'Is Boston a rich place, Ma?'

'The richest.'

'What was the plot?'

'I'm coming to that. First, they stole a small ship. Then they set off sailing around the Isle of Shoals. When they saw a passenger ferry crossing the river, young Rachel would start calling out, "Help us! Oh, help us! We're sinking!"'

'They were sinking?' Jem frowned.

'No! That was just a trick. But with Rachel being young and pretty the passenger ship never suspected her. The crew pulled alongside, Rachel and George climbed aboard ... and that's when they pulled out pistols and knives. They told the passengers to hand over all their purses and watches and rings and silk clothes.'

'Did they wear masks, Ma?' Jem asked with a puzzled scowl.

'No, son, that's the nasty part. They didn't care if the rich folk saw who was robbing them. Because the rich folk wouldn't live to tell the tale!'

'They shot them all!' Jem cried.

'No. Rachel and George got back on their own ship,

blasted the passenger ship below the waterline and left it to sink ... with all the people on board.'

'That's cruel,' Jem croaked.

'After a couple of years George went out alone and he was washed away in a storm,' Meg Hawkwood said.

'Served him right,' Jem nodded.

'And Rachel started sneaking onto ships in the harbour, robbing the cabins then creeping back on shore. She was good at it. But she was caught in the end.'

'What happened to her?'

'I was there in Boston when they hanged her.' Meg Hawkwood said. 'Hundreds of people turned out to watch. She had a good end.'

'What do you mean, Ma?'

'I mean she went quietly. No fussing or screaming. She said she deserved what she was getting. The crowd threw flowers, they let her drop and she was gone. That's how I'll go.'

Rachel Wall, the river pirate, was hanged in Boston in 1789 – just nine years before our story. So Meg Hawkwood could have seen the event. Mad Mac's tales were true ... except he wasn't there when they happened. A bit like a history teacher. Meg's tales were true AND she was there. Never trust a pirate (or a history teacher).

Jem thought about this for a while. 'But, Ma ... you *don't* deserve what you're getting! It's not the same at all. You were trying to save Lieutenant Darke ... and you did.

47

If you hadn't punched him then Mad Mac would have killed him!'

'Who would believe that?' Meg asked with a small, sad smile. 'Darke had just beaten my son. I had every reason to punch him ... and I did. That's what they'll think. It's war, Jem. Rules are always harder in war.'

'But we have to tell Captain Foley the truth!' the boy argued. 'He knows what Mac's like. He might believe you.'

She shrugged again. 'If we could prove Mac had murder in mind, he may be the one that they execute. But I know the way those men's minds work. He'd tell his friends to take their revenge. Grundle and Hope, Isaac and Jones would make sure both you and I vanished over the side some dark night. *I'm* hanged if I stay quiet ... we're *both* dead if I speak out. Now go and get on with your work before you get another beating.'

Jem stepped back into the hospital hold and swerved round a woman who was carrying an arm.

***

The sun was low and the air was starting to cool. Boats were taking French prisoners to the shores of Egypt and setting them free. 'We can't feed and care for all those prisoners,' Admiral Nelson had said.

A French sloop of war, less than half the size of *Goliath*, was towed alongside as a prize. 'She is called *Alerte*,' Captain Foley told the crew as they gathered on the deck. The men had been working all day to patch and repair the battered decks and masts, stitching sails, splicing ropes, stopping leaks and patching flags. News of a prize made them suddenly awake. Prizes meant money shared among the crew.

'When do we get paid?' Mac asked.

'The money will be paid when we get back to Portsmouth,' the captain told them.

'When will that be?' Isaac asked.

The captain spread his hands. 'The British Navy commands the seas ... but there are still some French warships out there. There may be more battles to be won. We can't all go home!' he said and laughed.

The crew didn't laugh.

Can you blame them? It's a bit like being told you've won the lottery, mate ... but you may not get paid till after you're dead.

'The *Alerte* needs to be taken back to our base in Portsmouth. She'll have British guns fitted and join the rest of the British Navy in Gibraltar. I suppose I can spare half a dozen men to take her to Portsmouth...'

'She's a fine 32-gun ship and only ten years old,' the Master Gunner said. 'She'll make us a fair bit of prize money.'

A lot of the crew looked interested again and muttered among themselves. It seemed most of *Goliath*'s crew wanted to sail *Alerte* back to Britain.

'Of course,' the captain sighed, 'Egypt is a rich country. They say the ancient kings are buried in massive tombs called pyramids. The tombs are stuffed with treasure. If you take *Alerte* back to England you may miss an even greater treasure.'

'That's right!' a gunner told his friends. 'That Napoleon wouldn't come all this way just to conquer a few natives ... especially natives that cut off your nose if they catch you.'

The others agreed. 'He came here for the treasures! They belong to us!'

Suddenly no one was so interested in *Alerte*. Mad Mac stepped forward. 'Captain Foley, sir ... I've commanded ships of this size before. I'd be happy to take her back to Portsmouth.'

'Well done, Macdonald. What crew will you need?'

'Why don't I just take a few sailors who know about sailing the coasts ... I mean I don't need Atlantic Ocean sailors do I? I guess I could make do with Grundle and Hope, Isaac and Jones.'

Grundle's mouth opened to object ... he was dreaming of pyramids of gold. But a sharp look from Mad Mac's eye silenced him. 'Aye, sir, we'll go with him.'

'So that's settled,' the captain said. 'You leave tomorrow. Crew dismissed!'

'Wait!' a voice cried from behind the men. Lieutenant Darke stepped up onto the deck from the hold below. He wore a bandage that was wrapped under his jaw and tied in a loop over the top of his hat. The men struggled to hide their laughter. 'Sorry, Captain, sir, but there is still the business of that woman to attend to!'

The captain sighed. Now the battle was over and

tempers had cooled he was hoping it would be forgotten. Darke marched over the deck and stood next to his captain. 'Bring the woman on deck,' Captain Foley ordered.

Meg Hawkwood strode on the deck, clanking chains as if they were light as thread. She stood beside Lieutenant Darke and smiled at him. The young officer took a sharp step backwards.

'Lieutenant Darke says that, on the night of the second of August, you struck him on the jaw. As you are aware, this is a serious offence Mrs Hawkwood.'

'I had to do it,' she said. She turned towards the silent crew. At last she found the face she was looking for. She stared straight at Mac the Pirate. She raised an eyebrow. One word from him would save her life and see him swing from the top mast.

The pirate just gave a tiny smile.

'It was a foolish action, Mrs Hawkwood, Why did you do it? Give me a good reason and I may be able to give you a less severe sentence?' the captain said, almost begging.

But Lieutenant Darke cut in, 'She did it because I struck her whelp of a son.'

Meg Hawkwood stepped towards the officer and raised her hands. 'My only mistake was that I didn't finish you off!'

Captain Foley stepped in front of her, 'Really, Mrs Hawkwood, you cannot continue to threaten His Majesty's Officers. I have no choice!' He took a deep breath. 'By the power invested in me as commander of this crew, I must

sentence you to hang from the yardarm...'

'Excuse me, sir,' Mad Mac said quietly. 'You have the power of life and death over this crew.'

Foley frowned. 'I know. That's what I said...'

'Ah, but Mrs Hawkwood is *not* a member of the crew. She is not on the ship's list of serving men. The crew share their food with her and she repays us with needlework at sea and working as a powder monkey in battle. But she is *not* under your orders ... in the law ... is she, sir?'

Foley's tight, white face broke into a slow smile. 'Hmm ... you might be right, Seaman Macdonald.'

'Oh, I say sir,' Lieutenant Darke said. 'You can't take a seaman's word for it. She hit me. She hit me on the chin. Look at the bruise. It hurt!'

'Not as much as the men who lost arms and legs and eyes and guts in the battle, Lieutenant,' Captain Foley said. 'It is my order that she be set free.'

'Oh, but sir, you can't do that!' the officer cried.

'*Can't*, Lieutenant? Are you telling me what I can and can't do on my own ship?'

'No ... but ... I meant...'

'Do you know the punishment for refusing to obey your captain? The rope is already rigged to the spar. Would you like to have a taste of it around *your* neck, Lieutenant Darke?'

Darke's face turned red as the sunset sky behind him. 'No, sir.'

'No, sir,' the captain said quietly. 'Now, Mrs Hawkwood, that gives me a problem of what to do with you. I can't punish you ... but I can't let you stay on my ship to attack any officer who slaps your son. Shall I put you ashore to be carved up by the tribesmen?'

'Yes, sir!' Meg Hawkwood laughed. 'Give me a cutlass and we'll see who does the carving!'

Before Captain Foley could reply Mad Mac stepped forward. 'Excuse me, sir, but I've been thinking ... maybe five is a small crew for a sloop of war after all – especially if we get into a fight with a Frenchie. Mrs Hawkwood could be useful – steering, being our powder monkey, patching sails. How about we take her with us?'

The captain turned to the woman. 'Well?'

'So long as I can take my Jem,' she said.

'That's agreed then,' Captain Foley told the crew. '*Alerte* sails tomorrow morning. Crew dismissed.'

Jem stood by his mother as her chains were removed. The pirate sidled up to her. 'You gave up all the treasures of Egypt, Mac?' she said.

He said quietly, 'The pyramids are empty. And any Egyptian treasure has to be shared among hundreds of men. No ... what I have in mind will bring us a much better fortune. A *real* fortune.'

He winked.

How did the one-eyed man wink? With his empty eye? In which case it wasn't a wink. Or with his good eye ... in which case it was a blink? I don't know.

WINE AND WOMEN

Saturday 4 August 1798

As the new crew of the French sloop *Alerte* climbed aboard her they could still smell the scent of smoke in her sails.

Grundle and Hope, Isaac and Jones checked the ropes and masts and lockers for damage. They were four happy men for the first time since they'd be press-ganged. Mad Mac strode across the poop deck like proud captain. The warm wind blew his wild grey hair like dandelion seeds.

Meg Hawkwood went into the ship's galley and found the food and fresh water. 'The French left enough to feed a crew of fifty,' she told her son. 'And here we have a crate of good French wine.'

'The crew will like that,' Jem said.

'No, they won't,' Meg told him. She climbed to the deck and called up to the *Goliath* that loomed above them. 'Send a rope down ... we have a crate of French wine that Captain Foley will like.'

As the wine was hauled up onto the warship, Jem asked, 'Why did you do that, Ma?'

'Because pirates and strong drink don't mix. Did you ever hear the story of Blackbeard and Israel Hands?'

'Whose hands?'

'Israel Hands ... he was one of Blackbeard's most trusted crew members. Blackbeard and Hands sat around a table supping wine one night. Blackbeard drank more and more till the wine heated his brain. He decided to play a little trick on Hands. He took out his pistol and fired it under the table.'

'That must have scared Israel Hands!' Jem laughed.

But Meg Hawkwood just scowled. 'He shot Hands in the knee. The man was lucky not to lose his leg. For the rest of his miserable life he struggled to limp along. *That's* what wine does to pirates and *that's* why we're better off without it on this ship.'

Jem nodded.

'And you'll have heard of Sir Henry Morgan?'

'Yes, Ma. He wrecked so many Spanish treasure ships the king made him governor of Jamaica. He was a great pirate!'

Meg snorted. 'A great pirate but a terrible sailor. He sailed one ship onto rocks and it sank. He had to cling to the rocks and wait to be rescued. He didn't seem so great then. And he let his men get so drunk on another ship they went down to the powder room with candles.'

'They shouldn't have done that!' Jem cried. He knew it was the first rule of the powder monkeys.

Mrs Hawkwood shrugged. 'They went looking for more wine in the hold. One of the sailors knocked a candle over ... well, you can guess what happened next?'

'The ship blew up?'

'Sent two hundred and fifty sailors to meet their maker,' Meg nodded. 'Sir Henry Morgan was lucky to escape with his life.'

'I bet that taught him not to drink,' Jem laughed.

'No, son. Pirates are too stupid to learn lessons like that. He drank more and more and in the end it killed him. Remember the song?' she said and sang it softly...

Fifteen men on a dead man's chest
Yo ho ho and a bottle of rum
Drink and the devil had done for the rest
Yo ho ho and a bottle of rum.
The mate was fixed by the bosun's pike
The bosun brained with a marlinspike
And cookey's throat was marked just like
It had been gripped by fingers ten;
And there they lay, all good dead men...'

'Pirates and liquor never mix. Remember that son.'

'I will, Ma,' the boy said. Then he stopped. 'Why, Ma? Why do I have to remember that? I mean I'm never going to be a pirate! Pirate days are finished. Even Mad Mac says so.'

Meg Hawkwood gripped her son by his skinny shoulders. 'It's too late, son. You already are a pirate. Why do you think Mad Mac offered to take this ship to England?'

57

'For the prize money, Ma.'

The woman shook her head sadly.

'The Navy buys the *Alerte* for a fair price and the sailors share the prize money, yes?'

'Yes, Ma.'

'Who gets it?'

'We do!'

'How much?'

'I – I don't know.'

'The crews of every ship in sight of *Alerte* when she surrendered ... five thousand sailors I reckon.'

Jem's face fell. 'That's not much for each of us.'

'Oh, it's worse,' his ma told him. 'A quarter of the money goes to the captains ... another half of the money goes to the officers ... and all the common sailors like Grundle and Hope, Isaac and Jones, have to share the last quarter. A pound or two if they are lucky.'

'That's not fair,' the boy said.

Jem could be right. A few dozen captains and officers get three-quarters of the prize for a captured ship. A few share a lot. A thousand sailors share a quarter. A lot share a little. Not fair. It's enough to make you want to punch a lieutenant on the jaw ... though you would hang for it. Sailors had to just take the money and grumble ... which they did.

'Mac didn't take this job for the prize money. Oh, no, the Mediterranean is swarming with trading ships. He told me his plan. Most of those ships have never seen a pirate. We can sail west and take a little from every trader we meet ... a sort of tax. By the time we get back to England we have a tidy little fortune ... we sell the treasure and we sell the ship ... and remember, we only have to share it between the seven of us.'

'It'll be dangerous,' Jem breathed.

His mother threw back her head and laughed. 'As dangerous as fighting the French? No! We stop unarmed traders – we take a little of their cargo. We don't sink them, like Rachel Wall, we don't murder them, like William Fly.'

'No, but if the Navy catches us they'll hang us,' Jem moaned.

'Jem. What are the Navy doing?'

'Fighting the French.'

'Do they have time to worry about a little pirate ship?'

'No, Ma.'

'We'll make a little pot of money and we'll settle back in England. I can open a tailor shop making clothes for gentlemen. And I've always wanted to own a tavern, but I would have to find a good pot man. And you ... what would you like to do, Jem?'

The boy stroked the side of the *Alerte*. 'Build ships, Ma.'

'There you are then! We have our dreams. A little bit of piracy will pay for them ... so long as we don't hang first.'

'How do we make sure we don't hang, Ma?'

Meg smiled. 'We learn from the pirates of the past ... we don't make their mistakes ... and we've started by unloading that wine.'

Suddenly Mad Mac appeared on the sunlit deck. 'What's in that crate they're hauling up on *Goliath*?'

'Biscuits, Captain Macdonald,' Meg Hawkwood sighed. 'Full of worms. Those poor French sailors were eating rotten biscuits. But I've found the food the officers ate on this ship. You'll eat well, Captain Macdonald, as long as I'm in charge of the galley here.'

Mad Mac raised his curved nose to sniff the sea air. 'Captain Macdonald ... I like the sound of that! Captain Macdonald! Grundle and Hope, Isaac and Jones!' he cried.

'Yes, Mac?'

'From now on you call me Captain Macdonald. Understand?'

'Yes, Mac.'

'Now, cast off, you scurvy knaves. Avast and belay there!'

The crew used poles to push themselves out of the shadow of the *Goliath*.

The wind caught the foresail and *Alerte* drifted into the deep emerald water that was still stained with charred wood and littered with slivers of ships. The crew of *Goliath* waved and cheered. 'See you again when you bring us back our prize money!' someone shouted.

But one figure stood alone on the poop deck, the knot on his bandage flapping on top of his head. His looks were as dark as his name. Lieutenant Darke muttered, 'I'd like to hang the lot of you ... and one day I will.'

***

Admiral Pierre-Charles-Jean-Baptiste-Silvestre de Villeneuve stood on the foredeck of the French warship *William Tell*, and placed a telescope to his eye. 'Malta ahead. Let's land and get supplies.'

> Amazing! If every French sailor had a name that long then the William Tell would have sunk under the weight. What's the heaviest name YOU'VE ever come across? I once knew a man called Stout.

The ship's captain, Fontaine, nodded. He was a small man with a weary face and sad eyes. 'What then, sir?'

The admiral stared fiercely ahead. 'Only two of our ships escaped Abukir Bay and that devil, Nelson,' he said. 'The French fleet is ruined. The Généreux has gone back to Toulon. But we can fight on.'

The captain coughed into his hand. 'We can't fight the whole British fleet, sir.'

Admiral Villeneuve looked at the man sourly. 'The British won't just sit there off the coast of Egypt, Captain, waiting for Napoleon to surrender. They will go back to Gibraltar or Portsmouth for food, gunpowder, fresh water, fresh crew.'

'Yes, sir.'

'And they won't sail away from Egypt together ... as a fighting fleet ... will they?'

'I wouldn't think so, sir.'

'I wouldn't think so either, Captain Fontaine. They will take it in turns. One or two ships at a time. And that is how we will fight them. As they try to sail across the Mediterranean we will be waiting for them ... and we'll destroy them, one ship at a time. Divide and conquer. We have eighty guns and six hundred men. When we capture a British warship we will have two ships ... then we will capture more and more!'

The captain chuckled. 'Pick them off one at a time ... like pirates, sir.'

Admiral Villeneuve managed a smile. 'Like pirates, Captain Fontaine. We will be waiting and we will take our revenge. Revenge for our friends who died at Abukir. Revenge for General Napoleon Bonaparte. But above all, revenge for the people of France. We didn't slice off all those noble heads and get our freedom just to have it taken away by a bunch of stinking Englishmen.'

'No, sir.'

'When we capture Nelson I will have the honour of putting his filthy neck on the guillotine myself!' he cried.

This would have been terribly cruel. Poor Admiral Nelson was only 166 cm tall. Without his head he'd have been tiny. In fact he wouldn't have been able to see where he was going. If you HAVE to chop off someone's head then pick on someone tall. Please.

The captain looked at him with a nervous smile. 'Of course, sir.'

***

Meanwhile, on the Alerte...
'The Frenchies didn't leave a drop of wine on the ship?' Mad Mac roared as he sat at the table in his cabin with a fine meal of stewed beef and cabbage and fresh-baked bread ... without a beetle or a worm in sight.

You know what they say? What's worse than finding a worm in your bread? Answer: finding half a worm in your bread. Think about it.

'No, Captain Macdonald,' Jem sighed as he placed a fine silver spoon beside the fine china plate. 'Ma thinks they must have thrown it overboard before they surrendered *Alerte*.'

'What a waste!' Mac groaned. 'Never mind. Sit down lad while I eat my meal and I'll tell you my plans to make your mother the richest woman in Nelson's Navy.'

'Yes, sir.'

'Captain Black Bart taught me this trick...'

'Not Black*beard*?' the boy asked.

'No. Black Bart. He was probably Blackbeard's brother,' Mad Mac said as he filled his mouth with bread and spooned in stew to follow.

You know what I'm going to say, don't you? Black Bart died in 1722 – seventy-six years before our story. Another big Mac whopper. Bart was ruthless and set fire to a slave ship – with 80 slaves trapped on board – when the captain wouldn't pay a ransom. But he was a holy man. He never attacked anyone on a Sunday – and he said prayers on board his ship. Maybe, 'Please God, send me lots of rich ships to rob.' We don't know. And we don't know God's answer either.

'Black Bart sailed up to merchant ships ... and the merchant ships sailed away as fast as they could. Black Bart knew they were scared of him and his scurvy crew. So he got his men and painted their faces white and their lips and cheeks red. He put them in silk dresses they'd captured and what did they look like?'

'Like right idiots?' Jem guessed.

Mad Mac choked on his food. 'No, you ignorant cur! They looked like *women*. He put his fake women in a boat and sent them over to the merchant ship. "Help! We need help!" the pirates cried into their hankies ... that hid their faces when they got closer.'

'Ah!' Jem nodded. 'And once they got on the merchant ship they pulled out their pistols and cutlasses.'

'Exactly! If the merchant crew didn't hand over their treasures then Black Bart's crew shot them, one by one, till they gave in!'

'Nasty,' Jem shuddered.

'You'll get used to it,' Mad Mac promised.

'Used to what?'

The captain leaned forward and grabbed the boy by the front of his shirt. He fixed him with his glittering eye. 'We don't need to dress up Grundle and Hope, Isaac and Jones as women. We already have a woman on board,' he explained.

'My ma?'

'Your ma. No one will think she is a ruthless pirate. And she needs another helpless-looking person in the rowing boat. A young lad. But a young lad who will shoot them between the eyes if the merchants try to argue.'

'Me?' Jem squeaked.

'You, lad! You are Captain Mac's perfect pirate.'

'Oh,' Jem said.

POEM AND 'PEACHY FACE'

Tuesday 7 August 1798

Grundle and Hope, Isaac and Jones took a rest from setting the sails and sat on a hatch at the front, sweating in the Mediterranean sun.

'It's hard work, sailing a sloop of war with just four of us,' Grundle grumbled.

'We have the woman and the boy to help us too,' Hope reminded him.

'But not the captain,' weedy Jones moaned.

'He's up on the mast on lookout. I suppose someone has to,' Hope said cheerfully. Even *his* dough face was turning brown after weeks in the summer sun.

'Heh!' weasel-faced Isaac cackled. 'You could say he's ... *keeping an eye out* for other ships.'

Grundle and Jones chuckled. Hope said, 'He already *has* an eye out.'

Isaac sighed a weasel sigh. 'It was a joke, Hope ... never mind.'

'As soon as he spots a ship we'll be rich. We sell this ship *and* a prize cargo, right?' Jones asked.

'Yes. And we're rich.'

'But we have to share it among us,' Jones complained. 'The captain gets *two* shares ... pirate rules. So each of us gets a seventh.'

'What does that mean?' dough-faced Hope asked.

Grundle sighed and took seven ship's biscuits and placed them on the hatch. 'Suppose we capture a ship and she has seven sacks of sugar on board. Here they are...'

'Sacks of sugar?' Hope frowned. 'They look like ship's biscuits.'

'No, Hope, *pretend* they are sacks of sugar. Each biscuit is a bag of sugar. They are worth a lot of money.'

'We're rich!'

'Ah!' Isaac put in, waving a warning finger. 'But Captain Mac takes two bags, ' he said scooping up two biscuits. 'I take one ... Grundle takes one ... Jones takes one ... and Meg Hawkwood takes one. What does that leave you, Hope?'

Hope stared at the hatch. 'One rotten ship's biscuit.'

'It's a bag of sugar.'

'Oh, yes ... one bag of sugar,' Hope nodded, as if he understood. 'Not much is it?'

'Not for the risk we're taking! Remember what happened to Captain Kidd?' Isaac cried.

'Who could forget it?' Jones nodded.

'I could forget it,' Hope said.

'They caught him and hanged him. But they didn't bury him,' Grundle said. 'And you know what happens to poor souls that don't get a proper burial?'

'No.'

'They can't go to heaven. Their tormented spirits are left to wander the earth, looking for rest.'

'Ooooh! Ghosties!' Hope gasped.

'But to make sure Kidd *never* got any rest they took his corpse down and covered it in tar so it wouldn't rot. And then they hanged it in a cage at Boston Harbour.'

'What for?'

'So all the sailors could see it ... like a warning of what happens if you turn to piracy,' Jones nodded.

'His corpse is probably still there now – ninety years after he was hanged!' Isaac said. 'I remember when I was a lad, my ma told me the poem they wrote about the corpses of Captain Quelch and his crew – they were hanged at Boston too.' Isaac half-closed his weasel eyes and recited it...

'You pirates, who against God's laws did fight,
Have all been hanged, which is very right.
Some of you were old and some were very young,
And on the Boston gallows you were hung.'

Oh, I know it wasn't a very good poem. But it can't have been easy – writing several pages ... on sailors hung in cages ... by the landing stages ... sitting there for ages ... no more pirate rages ... hanging is their wages.

'And then,' Jones said, 'if they were sent off to be buried they'd be buried face-down so their spirits wouldn't have a clue where they were when they woke up dead.'

'Still,' Isaac argued, 'it's better than what they did in Jamaica. They hung you up in the cage *alive*. They just left you to die slowly in the sun. Horrible.'

'Yes, yes,' Grundle said. 'The point is, we are risking all that punishment for one sack of sugar. If there were fewer of us to share it out then we'd each get more ... I mean, if that Meg Hawkwood fell overboard before we got back to Portsmouth, we'd get her share!'

Hope frowned. 'Wouldn't young Jem get her share?'

Grundle's face turned fierce. 'Not if the lad went overboard with her! Heh! Heh!'

'That's nasty,' Hope said.

'That's what pirates do,' Grundle said ... and wondered if Hope might just happen to vanish over the side before their journey ended.

It was almost as if Hope had read his mind. Hope said, 'At least I know you can't throw me over the side,' Hope chuckled.

'Why not?'

'Because I can't swim!'

***

Grundle sometimes worried about Hope. He would have been more worried if he knew his captain was letting more of his treasure slip away...

Jem had climbed to the top of the mast to join Captain Macdonald in the look-out platform ... the crow's nest.

That's a funny name for a look-out post. Yes, I know the bowl on the top of the mast looks like the nest of a crow at the top of a tree. What I mean is, you don't see many crows at sea. You see seagulls. If I had a pirate ship I'd tell my lookout, 'Get yourself up to the gull's nest, you lubber!'

'Aharrrrgh, Jem lad,' the captain grinned. 'Come to keep your old captain company?'

'Not really,' the boy said. 'I came to tell you I want a share of the treasure when we get it.'

'What?' the captain cried. 'Don't go saying things like that when I'm up here! I could fall out onto the deck and kill meself. How would you manage then?'

'Pretty well,' Jem told him.

Mad Mac pulled a knife from his belt and waved it under Jem's nose. 'Pirate rules say you get your ears cut off if you're cheeky to the captain.'

Jem shook his head. 'No they don't. You just made that up. Pirate rules say anyone who takes a woman or a boy on board will be killed. You have got *both*, Captain.'

'Ah, well...'

'I'm taking the same risk as you so I should have an equal share of the treasure,' the boy reminded him.

The captain nodded. 'Aye! I know that's one of Black Bart's rules!'

'So I want a share of the treasure,' Jem said calmly.

'What? You're not a man! If we give you a share we'll have to share it eight ways ... two parts for me and six for the rest of you. Grundle and Hope, Isaac and Jones won't like that.'

'Grundle and Hope, Isaac and Jones aren't going to board the merchant ships and take all the risks. Me and Ma will be doing that. So you give me and Ma a share each and we'll do it!'

Captain Macdonald's mouth moved but he couldn't find the words. 'I'll think about it,' he said finally.

Jem shrugged. 'Then you'd better think quickly.'

'Why?'

'Because there's a merchant ship half a league off the larboard bow, Captain.'

'What? Where? There! Look! Our first prize! Quick!' he said. The captain called down, 'Get the ship's boat ready! Merchant ship ahead! Right, lad, you know the plan.'

Jem didn't move. 'I know the plan but I am not going till you agree ... there are seven members of this crew. A magnificent seven.'

'I like that,' the captain nodded. 'A secret seven!'

'So, I get a share?'

'I could kill you,' the man hissed.

Jem laughed. 'And my ma would kill *you*. You saw what she did to Lieutenant Darke ... you saw it better than anyone. Ma is as good a fighter as any man ... and probably better than an old man like you. So, am I number seven?' he asked and spat in the palm of his hand. He held it out.

Captain Macdonald spat in his own hand and shook the boy's hand.

This is a disgusting habit and spreads germs. But it is a bit like blood brothers letting their blood mix. If YOU have a close friend don't try blood OR spit ... try something cleaner. Fresh custard is very nice.

'Number seven,' Mad Mac said. 'Now get to work!'

***

Admiral Nelson had a wide bandage around his head. The captains of each of the ships in the fleet sat around the table in Nelson's cabin.

'So, gentlemen, we have won a great victory. The French prisoners have been put ashore and packed off to find General Napoleon Bonaparte.'

'If the tribesmen don't find them first!' one of the captains said and the others laughed. Even Nelson managed a smile.

'We can start sending ships back to Gibraltar and England to be repaired and give the crews a break,' the admiral said. 'If one ship leaves each month it won't leave us too weak. The first ship to sail home will take the news of this victory. I've chosen *Leander* and Captain Edward Berry to go first. She's the one with the most damage.'

The captains nodded. Captain Foley said, 'She's only got half of her fifty guns in action. What if Captain Berry meets a French battleship on the way home?'

Nelson spread his hands. 'It's a chance we have to take ... but I feel the French won't have the stomach for another fight.'

***

The ship's boat was lowered down the side of *Alerte*. Jem and Meg Hawkwood slid down ropes into the boat and started rowing towards the merchant ship. Their belts were packed with knives and pistols that dug into Jem's ribs with every stroke of the oars.

'Ma?'

'Yes, son?'

'Do we really have to shoot these people ... even if they aren't carrying weapons?'

'No, son. That would be a big mistake,' she said as she pulled powerfully. If we murder some of them the others will sail off and find the Navy. They'll hunt us down. And *that* would mean we'd have to kill them all. I may punch the odd naval officer ... if I think it'll save his life ... but I'm not a murderer, Jem.'

'No, Ma ... but even if we don't hurt anyone they'll send the Navy after us,' Jem argued.

'Maybe ... or maybe not if we are clever about it. If we rob them but don't let them know they've been robbed!'

'How will we do that, Ma?'

'When we get on board let me do the talking and we'll see,' she said and bent her back to pull on the oars.

The merchant ship had lowered her sails and they had soon rowed across to her. 'Ahoy there!' Meg called. 'Thanks for waiting, shipmates!' she called up.

It was a warm day but the man who looked down from the ship's rail was wearing a fine green coat, a heavy white wig and a cocked hat.

'Greetings, lady. You're not in trouble, are you?'

'Not at all!' Meg laughed as they bumped against the side of the merchant ship and stowed their oars.

A sailor threw down a rope and they tied their rowing boat so it didn't drift away. Meg and Jem then used the rope to haul themselves onto the deck of the merchant ship.

Alerte stood a pistol shot away and nine pirate eyes watched silently for the signal to move closer and board their victim.

'Welcome on board the *Peachy Face*,' the man in the green suit said.

'The *what*?' Meg gasped.

The man blushed. 'My wife wanted me to call it after her ... well, my pet name for her. What could I do?'

Meg shook her head. 'I'm Meg Merryweather of *Alerte*,' she said and jerked a thumb at Jem. 'This is just a cabin boy.'

'And I am Captain Swift of the *Peachy* ... erm ... what

can I do for you?'

Meg pressed her hands together and smiled like an angel. 'No, Captain Swift. It is what *I* can do for *you*. I've come to help you! Let's go into the cool of your cabin and talk about it.'

Nine pirate eyes on board *Alerte* watched her disappear. Five pirate brains wondered ... what on earth was Meg Hawkwood up to?

SWIFT AND SHANTY

'**N**ow, Captain Swift!' Meg Hawkwood cried. 'I'll bet you are truly pleased to see us.'

'Am I?' asked the round-faced captain in the green suit.

'And, yes, you are *right*, I would love a pot of your cool ale ... rowing over here was warm work,' the woman said.

'Of course!' the captain said with a nervous smile. He ordered a sailor to fetch a drink.

Meg took out a sheet of parchment, a quill pen and a pot of ink. 'I'll just note down your details while we wait ... *Peachy Face* ... Captain Swift ... first name?'

'Samuel.'

'Really? One of my favourite names ... Samuel,' she said and patted his cheek. 'Now ... Samuel ... where are you sailing to and from?'

'Who are you?' the captain asked. 'I mean, you could be pirates or anything!'

Meg threw back her head, shook her thick red hair and laughed. 'Oh, Samuel! You are a funny man. I'll bet your Peachy Face wife never stops laughing!'

'Ah ... well...'

'Do we *look* like pirates?' she smiled.

'I don't know ... I've never met one,' he shrugged.

'I have,' Meg said, suddenly serious. 'Ugly men with sun-baked faces and sword scars, with wooden legs, with parrots, with eye patches...'

'Parrots with eye patches?'

'No ... the pirates have eye patches ... the parrots don't ... unless they are very unlucky parrots that got in a fight with a seagull and lost an eye, of course.'

'Of course.'

'Does the boy here look like a pirate?'

'No, not at all...'

'We are from His Majesty's government. We work for the customs department,' she said.

'I'm not a smuggler!' Captain Swift squawked ... a bit like a parrot in a fight with a seagull.

'No, Samuel! Oh, no! We never said you were! You are no more a smuggler than I am a pirate,' the woman laughed. 'I mean you may have the odd barrel of brandy stowed away that you forget to tell the customs officer about ... but I'm sure that is not for sale.'

'Isn't it?'

'No. It's for you and Peachy Face to enjoy by the fireside when you get home,' she said softly and gave him a gentle dig in the ribs with her elbow. 'So, Samuel, what port are you out of?'

'The port of Tyre,' he said.

Meg Hawkwood made a note.

'On what date did you leave?'

'Monday the sixth.'

Meg's face fell. 'Oh, dear! You won't have heard about the new customs duties then? Oh, poor Samuel! No wonder you were confused when I came on board.'

He smiled weakly. 'Just a bit.'

'Let me explain. Admiral Nelson has just won a mighty battle at the mouth of the River Nile,' she said.

'Yes, news of that had reached Tyre before we left,' Samuel Swift nodded. 'What a great man. They say they will make him *Lord* Nelson when he gets home to England.'

'I'm sure they will. The trouble is the British fleet needs more ships and we need them quickly. We need to guard the Nile ... keep Napoleon Bonaparte trapped ... but we also have to patrol the French ports. We need to make sure the French don't send a *new* fleet from Toulon or somewhere, don't we?'

'Do we?'

'Well *you* do!'

'Do I?'

'Of course! It's YOU we have to protect! You great traders. Without you, Britain is nothing. Admiral Nelson is fighting for YOU, Samuel Swift. Nelson will keep the seven seas safe for magnificent men like you. Nelson may get the medals and the glory but we all know it is the masters of the oceans, the Samuel Swifts of the seas, that really matter.'

'You're right,' the captain said, He raised his hat and wig and used a fine handkerchief to mop his bald head.

'And that's why King George said it is only fair that people like YOU pay a small extra tax ... the money will go to building the new ships Nelson needs,' Meg finished.

Captain Swift frowned. 'We already pay taxes ... we pay duty on this cargo when it's landed.'

'Ah, I know, but the new tax is only ten per cent,' she explained.

'How much?'

'One part in ten goes to us and you get to keep ninety per cent! How *generous* is that? *Ninety* per cent for you! Why ... it makes you and Peachy Face a rich couple doesn't it? King George is giving you *ninety* per cent!'

'When you put it like that...'

'Of course you will land in port ... where are you headed?'

'Bristol.'

'You will land in Bristol, you will be desperate to throw yourself into the face of Peachy Arms ... but the customs officers will stop you.'

'They will?'

'Oh, yes! They have to inspect your ship, look at your cargo and work out ten per cent. Only *then* can you unload it and sell it. If there's a queue of ships waiting you could be held up for days!'

'I could,' Captain Swift nodded.

'So, we are here to help. We will do the job here and now. We'll take ten per cent of your cargo and send you on your way.'

'That's a good idea!' Swift said.

'So what are you carrying?' Meg asked and raised her pen.

'A hundred and twenty bales of silk from China,' Captain Swift said. 'Ten sacks of Indian tea and a few boxes of spice.'

Meg nodded and went to the cabin door. She placed her fingers between her lips and gave a sharp whistle that scared away every fish for miles. Grundle and Hope, Isaac and Jones looked across and she waved for them to pull alongside *Peachy Face*.

'Get your crew to start unloading twelve bales of silk, a sack of tea and a box of spices.'

'Yes, Miss Merryweather,' Swift said and hurried off ... swiftly ... to obey.

Meg winked at Jem. 'See? No need to hurt anyone. There's no need to murder for Mac. And they won't dash straight to the nearest port to report the robbery.'

'That's clever, Ma,' the boy said.

'I'm twice as clever as Mad Mac,' she said. 'But he's useful to have around. A few more ships like this and we'll head home to sell our loot.'

Captain Swift came back, smiling. 'It's all being unloaded. Do you want any of our brandy?'

'No!' Meg said sharply. 'My crew don't drink!'

'Don't drink?!'

'Well ... they drink *water* of course. But no strong spirits.'

Captain Swift sighed. 'You have a good crew ... though they look a little ... erm ... *rough* ... if I may say?'

'They have all been rescued from jail,' Meg explained. 'They have turned their back on crime and only want to help mighty merchants like you sail safely,' she said. 'Of course they would not say no to a little gold. Have you much on board?'

'Just a hundred pounds to buy some barrels of wine in Spain on the way home.' He reached into a chest on the cabin table and pulled out a leather purse.

Meg nodded. 'King George will take ten percent of that,' she said.

'Ten pounds!' Captain Swift gasped and clutched his purse to his chest.

She leaned forward. 'King George doesn't know you have a hundred pounds,' she murmured. 'I'll tell him you just had eighty ... give me eight pounds and I'll say no more.'

The captain handed over the money quickly then pushed the purse back in the chest and locked it.

Meg wrote a list of the goods she had stolen and signed the bottom of the sheet. 'There you are, Captain. Look after this document. It will tell the customs officers in Bristol you've already paid your war tax!'

'Thank you, thank you, thank you,' the captain said and held the sheet carefully. 'It has been a pleasure doing business with you,' he said.

'The pleasure was *all* mine, Samuel. And, when you get home, please be sure you give my love to Peachy Face,' Meg said.

'I will, Miss Merryweather, I will.'

Meg and Jem climbed down onto *Alerte* and waved farewell to Captain Samuel Swift and *Peachy Face*.

***

'You did *what*?' Captain Macdonald raged as *Alerte* sailed away from *Peachy Face*.

'Let him keep most of his cargo,' Meg said quietly and explained.

'What sort of pirate are you?' the captain sneered.

'A very clever one. All the pirates you know are dead. What killed them?'

'A rope round the neck, a bullet in the brain or a cutlass making them gutless usually,' Grundle said.

They could die a hundred different ways of course. Black Bart had his throat torn by a cannonball. Captain George Lowther was shipwrecked on a desert island and shot himself. William Lewis was stabbed by his own crew. As Black Bart liked to say, 'A short life but a merry one.' Or 'A short life but a merry where's me throat gone?'

'No,' Meg told the crew. 'It was greed that killed them. Take a little from a sailor and he grumbles. Take *everything* he has and he wants revenge,' the woman went on.

'That's why we should kill them,' Isaac said savagely.

Meg sighed. 'Then we have the Navy hunting us down till they take us dead or alive. Anyway, I have a small present for you all,' she said and reached into a pocket of her dress. She pulled out eight golden sovereigns. 'Here you are ... two for Captain Macdonald – pirate rules – and one for each of us.'

'Even the boy?' Jones sniffed.

'The *boy* risked his life going on board the merchant ship. If it had all gone wrong, *you'd* have sailed off and left us, wouldn't you?'

'Suppose so,' Jones mumbled.

'But Jem and me would have been fish food by now. But if you think Jem doesn't deserve an equal share I'll throw his coin over the side,' the woman offered.

'No!' five of the magnificent seven cried.

'There you are, Jem ... your first loot as a pirate.'

'Thanks, Ma,' Jem said.

'We have a fine haul of silk, tea and spices ... now we need some sugar, some gold, some cheap cloth and maps.'

'Maps?'

'Very valuable are maps,' Captain Macdonald agreed. Suddenly he turned his fierce eye on Meg. 'Here! Why are *you* to be telling *me* what to steal?'

Meg gave him her special warm smile. 'Because I know how real pirates like you work. You can't sell a shipload of silk all in one go. And no use trying to sell silk if a port is looking to buy sugar. Much better to have lots of different things to sell at different ports.'

Mad Mac glared at the deck. 'I knew that,' he muttered.

'So let's head west towards Malta,' Meg said.

'I was going to say that,' Captain Macdonald said.

'I thought you might, Captain,' the woman nodded. 'Where there's an island there are traders coming and going all the time.'

And so they turned west again and sailed under a sun hot enough to shrink the planks of the deck. After their first victory Grundle and Hope, Isaac and Jones worked as hard as they ever had in their lives.

***

Saturday 18 August 1798

It was the next week, Wednesday, when they had sighted Malta. Three ships had fallen for Meg Hawkwood's tax tale and the hold of *Alerte* was filling up steadily. Even Captain Macdonald was starting to see how the woman's wit was making their fortune.

Off the coast of Malta the captain spotted another merchant ship.

'Looks like she's carrying wine barrels on the deck. We can always sell wine back in England,' Meg said. 'So long as the barrels stay sealed. No wine merchant will buy a barrel that has been opened. Take us towards her,' she ordered.

The men obeyed as if she were their captain.

The new ship had the name *Justice* painted on her stern. Meg gave the crew a friendly wave. They didn't wave back but looked at her curiously.

'Miserable lot,' she said to Jem. 'Must be from Hull. Let's get into the rowing boat.'

The crew of *Justice* lowered their sails and let Meg and Jem row alongside. They lowered a rope and the pirates climbed it. 'Good evening!' she cried happily.

The captain was a sour-faced man with long, ragged hair. He frowned and said, 'Bon soir, Madame.'

'What?' Meg said.

'It's French, Ma,' Jem muttered as the crew gathered round them in a circle.

'I know it's *French*... I just wonder *why* a Hull ship's captain is speaking French to me.'

Jem's face lit up. 'Because *Alerte* is a French sloop of war of course! He thinks we're Bonaparte's navy! No wonder they don't look very happy to see us!'

Meg nodded, 'Of course, son. Clever lad.'

'I think you're mistaken, Captain,' she said happily.

'What ... mistake I make?' he asked. He had a strong accent. A French accent.

Jem felt his knees turn as watery as the sea below. 'I think *we* made the mistake, Ma ... *this* is a French ship.'

'Ohhhh, dear,' Meg Hawkwood sighed. 'Oh dear, oh dear, oh dear.'

ROPE AND REVOLUTION

The French captain gave some orders to his crew and they ran off to obey. He turned to Meg and Jem and spoke in good English. 'Would you come into my cabin so we can discuss your business?'

He led the way into the cabin under the poop deck. The little room smelled of stale wine and sweat. 'Now, Madame, how can I help you?'

Meg sat on the bench that ran alongside the map table. 'We are tax collectors for ... for the great Emperor Napoleon Bonaparte.'

'Really?' the captain said.

'You may not have heard but Napoleon's fleet were defeated in Abukir Bay,' Meg went on.

The captain's face went stiff. 'The British cheated. They did not fight by the rules of war. They did not dare face the French cannon. Instead they sneaked behind like an assassin who stabs in the back.'

'They did,' Meg nodded. 'Those British are such cowards!'

'But *you* are English, are you not?'

'I *am* ... and so are my crew. But they all hate Admiral Nelson. Hate him. Don't you, Jem?'

'Hate him,' Jem said and nodded hard.

'But you are out here, a thousand miles from your home. You must be fighting for him!' the French captain said.

'Captain,' Meg Hawkwood said and leaned forward. 'What is your name?'

'De Nantes,' he told her. 'Raoul de Nantes.'

'Well, Raoul, you may have heard of the press gangs in Britain? They snatch men from the ports – ordinary fishermen and traders and force them to serve in Nelson's Navy? Well, the crew of *Alerte* are all pressed men.'

'So?'

'So ... as soon as they had a chance they jumped off the British ship and rowed across to *Alerte*,' the woman explained.

'In the middle of the battle?'

'Yes. Of course the *Alerte* was one of the few ships to escape from the cowardly British,' she went on. 'The French sailors were pleased to see us. And so was Napoleon!'

Raoul de Nantes blinked. 'You met Napoleon *himself*?'

'Oh, yes, a great man. So tall and handsome!' she sighed.

'Napoleon is a short man,' the Frenchman said. 'He is no taller than your Nelson.'

'I *know*!' Meg laughed. 'That's what I said! We met Napoleon ... so *small* and handsome. And such a great brain too! He came up with a wonderful scheme and that is why we are here.'

'This *scheme*,' the captain said and poured some watered-down wine into cups for Meg and Jem. 'What is it?'

'Napoleon knows how much the British hate this war. They hate King George and they want him to face the guillotine just like your King Louis. The British want their own revolution,' she smiled and sipped at the wine.

'They do? Then why are they going to war with us?' Captain de Nantes asked.

'That's our leaders ... the rich folk. They're afraid the ordinary British people will start chopping off heads. They want to smash your revolution and Napoleon.'

'And you?'

'We are the *real* people. We want a British revolution! As soon as we land back in Britain we'll buy arms for the poor.'

The French captain gave a smile as thin as a new moon. 'And I thought you were pirates!'

'No! We haven't come to rob your cargo. Napoleon gave us *Alerte* and told us to tax any French ships we met!'

'Tax?'

'You give us ten per cent of your cargo. We sell the cargo and raise money for a British peasant army,' Meg said happily.

Captain de Nantes nodded. 'Of course there will be a lot of blood. Are you ready for that?' he asked a little sadly. 'I was in Paris when the Terror was at its worst. I stood outside the prison where Queen Marie Antoinette was held prisoner with her son. The crowd called to her, "Look out of the window, Your Majesties and see what happens to the likes of you". Some people were waving a pole at the window. On the pole was a head. Its long fair hair was caked with blood and waved in the wind. Marie Antoinette knew that face. It was the Princess de Lamballe! Her friend!'

'That's cruel,' Jem said and shuddered.

'The princess had been beheaded. Her body had been dragged through the streets and the head was perched on a pole. Her heart had been ripped out and waved on the end of a sword,' Captain de Nantes said. 'I was there when King Louis XVI was executed ... and he died horribly.'

'I thought the guillotine was quick and painless,' Jem said.

'Not always,' the captain told him. 'Louis was laid face down on the guillotine and the executioner, Sanson, pulled the rope. The blade fell. The king screamed. His neck was so fat the blade failed to slice it off first time. It came off at a second attempt. A young guard, about eighteen years old, picked up the head for the crowd to see. "Long live the Revolution!" he cried. The crowd rushed forward to dip handkerchiefs in the blood.'

And some people say the pain didn't end there! They say the head stays alive for half a minute or more AFTER it's been chopped off. So you feel the pain of your nose hitting the basket. Creepy, eh?

'He probably deserved it,' Meg said, but she didn't sound so sure now.

'Is this what you want to see on the streets of London?'

'What happened to Queen Marie Antoinette?' Jem asked.

'I wasn't there but I heard the stories. She went to her death quite bravely. The guards didn't treat her too kindly. They arrived in her cell and tied her hands behind her back. She argued that king didn't have his hands tied when they executed him. They tied her anyway. They then had to untie her again so she could have a pee.'

'But did she die quickly?' Jem asked.

'They chopped her hair at the neck so it wouldn't get in the way of the guillotine. She was put into a cart and led through the streets of Paris. The guillotine was supposed to be quick – a couple of people a minute could be chopped. Yet it took them four long minutes to get Marie Antoinette ready. Can you imagine her terror in those minutes?'

Meg and Jem just nodded.

'As the queen stepped onto the platform she trod on the foot of the executioner and the man cried out in pain. So Marie Antoinette's famous last words were, "I beg your pardon, sir, I didn't do it on purpose." The executioner took off her white cap. She was almost bald. The crowd laughed and jeered at her for her ugliness. The blade came down, the head fell. A man picked up the head and waved it at the cheering, jeering crowd.'

Meg's sunburnt face was as pale as it could be. 'Horrible.'

'Their poor children were left as orphans. And you tell me that is what you want in Britain?' the captain said with that bitter smile.

'Yes,' Meg Hawkwood said in a whisper. She cleared her throat. 'Just give us Napoleon's tax and we will be on our way.'

The captain looked at her sadly. 'Madame, the executions were cruel. So I decided that when I execute someone it will be quick.'

'Who are you going to execute?' the woman asked with a frown.

'Why, you, of course,' Captain de Nantes said.

***

Meanwhile, on board Alerte...

Grundle and Hope, Isaac and Jones had watched as Meg and Jem climbed aboard the *Justice*. They waited for the order to pull alongside and unload a share of her cargo.

Captain Macdonald squinted at them from his position at the crow's nest. He watched Meg and Jem step into the captain's cabin. That part always made him uneasy. Then he watched the captain send a couple of sailors off to the main deck.

The voices of the sailors carried on the breeze. Strange voices. French voices. Mad Mac gave a grim grin. 'Let's see you talk your way out of that one, Meg Hawkwood,' he murmured to himself.

As the dangerous moments ticked by, Mac watched the French sailors working on a rope. They were binding one end of the rope in a loop. One of them put his foot in the loop and tested it. The binding held tight. He passed the end to the second sailor who put it between his teeth and began to climb the rigging. At the top spar of the mainsail he stopped, threw the loop over the spar and lowered it towards the deck.

Mac knew what he was looking at now. He had seen it many times before. It was a noose. He knew whose neck would be inside it soon. 'Oh, Mrs Hawkwood. Your polite pirate act doesn't always work.'

He scrambled down the rigging to the deck and gathered a pair of pistols from his cabin. He found some oiled cloth and wrapped up the pistols tightly. He jammed them into his belt along with a dagger.

Captain Macdonald stepped up to the rail on the larboard side. 'Where are you off to, Captain?' Jones asked.

'To do a bit of real pirating for a change,' he said. 'A pirate always helps a shipmate in distress,' he went on.

'Is that one of the pirate laws?' Isaac asked.

'It is now ... I just invented it,' his captain said. He stood on the rail, looked down into the cool, rippling water and dived.

***

'Why would you want to execute me?' Meg asked.

'Because you are a pirate,' Captain de Nantes said. 'Tell me, have you tried this trick on British ships?'

'Trick?' Meg said and raised her eyebrows.

'This nonsense about a tax? You may fool simple-minded British captains but I am *French*. And I know that the ship *William Tell* escaped the battle – but *Alerte* was captured. Your ship is a *British* ship. If you are fighting under the command of Admiral Nelson you are a spy ... and I will hang you. If you have stolen the ship so you can rob others, then you are a pirate. Either way, I hang you.'

'Have you ever seen a woman pirate?' Jem asked.

The French captain spread his hands. 'Women? They can be as cold in the blood as men. Who do you think carried the corpses away from the guillotine? The women. They loaded them on to a cart and took them off to the graves. And, when the cart stopped on the journey for a rest, the blood dripped to the ground. The women danced in the blood of their enemies. Ah, just because *Madame* is a woman doesn't mean she's not a pirate.'

Meg sighed. 'I can see you are too clever for me.'

'Wait!' Jem cried. 'You can't hang my ma!'

Captain de Nantes took off his hat and ran a weary hand through his ragged hair. 'Why not?'

'Because my father died in a battle last year. If you kill Ma then I'll be an orphan. That's cruel ... and you said you felt sorry for Marie Antoinette's orphans!'

'Hmmmm! Yes. You are right!' the captain cried. 'You would have to live a life of misery, alone and lonely. He stepped to the door of the cabin and called out, '*Une autre corde!*'

'There you are, my boy. I have ordered another rope. You can hang alongside your *maman*. You will never be lonely and miserable! A good idea?'

Jem glared at the man.

The captain took some cord from a drawer in the map

table and tied Meg Hawkwood's wrists behind her. Then it was Jem's turn. He looked out of the cabin door again. 'Ah, *voila*! The second noose is ready. Step forward.' He called out, 'Charles! Hang these pirates!'

He stood in the doorway just below the poop deck rail and watched as a large sailor grabbed the Hawkwoods roughly by the shoulders and marched them on to the deck.

'Sorry, we have no time for a priest to hear your prayers,' the captain said coldly. Jem's ankles were tied with cord and the rough rope slipped over his head.

'Say goodbye to each other,' the captain said.

Meg shuffled round around so she was facing Captain de Nantes. The sailors who stood beside her froze as stiff as mizzen masts. Meg's face split in a grin. 'One last request, Captain?'

'What is it?'

'Well, you know I wanted a tenth of your cargo?'

'Yes?'

'I have changed my mind ... since you have been so unkind.'

'What do you mean?'

'I mean I now want half of it. Or else.'

The Frenchman scowled at her. 'Or else what?'

'Or else my Captain Macdonald will fire that pistol he is holding to the back of your head and blow your brains all over your ship. Nice to see you, Captain Macdonald, sir!'

Raoul de Nantes turned slowly and found himself staring into the barrels of two pistols.

'And it is nice to see you, Meg Hawkwood. Having a little trouble, are you?'

'Not any longer, Captain Macdonald, sir!' she called back.

SWORD OF SURRENDER

Saturday 18 August 1798

Admiral Villeneuve stood next to the ship's captain on *William Tell* and scanned the sea with his telescope. At last he saw the ship his lookout had seen from the top of the mighty warship's mast.

As they drew closer he saw the British flag flying from the mast. 'Time for revenge, gentlemen,' he said.

Of course Admiral Villeneuve said it in French. That's because his crew understood French. I could tell you what he said in FRENCH if you want ... but you wouldn't understand ... unless you are a) very good at speaking French or b) French. So I won't bother. If you ARE a) very good at speaking French or b) French then I'm sorry.

Sailors ran to raise more sails and *William Tell* started to draw closer to the English ship. A French officer said, 'Looks like the little 50-gun ship that fired on the *Franklin*. I think her name is *Leander*.'

'She's trying to run from us,' Admiral Villeneuve said.

'Can't blame her,' Captain Fontaine snorted. 'We have 80 guns and *we* ran away before we were damaged.'

The Admiral scowled. 'We *retreated,* we didn't *run away*.'

'No, sir.'

'We saved our ship for a day like today when we could pick off the British ships one at a time.'

'The *Leander* is turning, sir,' the captain told him. 'Her crew must be crazy!'

'I think she's too damaged to escape from us. She may as well go down fighting,' Admiral Villeneuve said.

'She'll be attacking with the wind behind her.'

'That means she can choose the way we fight? We're just sitting here like target practice for her. How did you get us into this mess, Captain Fontaine?' the Admiral said with an explosion of rage like one of *William Tell*'s cannon.

'Sorry, sir,' the captain muttered. He leaned over the deck rail and called, 'Man the guns!'

The master gunner looked up. 'Starboard or larboard, sir?'

The captain stared hard at *Leander*. 'She's heading straight towards us ... she could go either side ... we'll have to have gunners ready at both sides. We don't want to make the same mistake our fleet made at Abukir Bay!'

The gunners ran to their posts as the powder monkeys scurried below. Swabbies cleared the decks and deck hands lowered the sails so the *William Tell* sat steady and ready in the swollen sea.

At the last moment *Leander* swung to the larboard side of *William Tell* and as she raced past she let loose a broadside of cannon. *William Tell* replied with an even more fierce blast – all her guns were in order and there were more of them.

Sails on *Leander* tore and ropes were ripped as she

raced by. Splinters of wood shot through the air like javelins. Men were speared and they fell bleeding to the decks. Swabbies picked them up and carried them below to the ship's doctor.

The wounded men were put in a line, some moaning and bleeding, some falling still and dead. The doctor and his helpers treated them one at a time, in order. That was the rule on British ships.

'Aha!' You cry. 'I'll bet Admiral Nelson didn't wait his turn in a queue when he was hit in the head at Abukir Bay.' Aha! I reply. You are wrong! He did. He moaned a lot and said he was dying, but he never said, 'Treat me first – I'm the admiral.'

Sailors cut away the snapped ropes above the decks. Carpenters patched the holes in the side and covered them in tar to keep out the water. Powder monkeys raced

below to fetch more gunpowder and gunners cleaned the guns while they waited to fire again.

On the French ship the sailors were doing just the same. *William Tell* was a bigger ship with more cannon but there were more men on board and more to be wounded by *Leander*'s guns. Only the men on her starboard side were untouched by death and injury. They knew their turn would come.

Captain Edward Berry turned *Leander* in a full, wide circle so she could attack *William Tell* a second time.

'This time she'll come down the starboard side!' Admiral Villeneuve cried and the powder monkeys ran to supply the gunners there. *Leander* charged in again ... and passed by the larboard side.

Again *Leander*'s guns sprayed death over the decks of *William Tell* and again her sails and rigging were shredded by the French ship's mighty gun power.

As the British ship circled for a third attack Admiral Villeneuve saw papers and boxes flung over the side of the British ship. 'Their captain is throwing his secret codes and messages overboard,' Villeneuve spat.

Captain Fontaine nodded. 'They must be pretty sure they are going to lose in the end then.'

The *Leander* was like a moth battering at a lantern glass. She came back again and again but each attack made her weaker and slower till at last a shot from *William Tell* brought down her mast. *Leander* slowed and wallowed in the water. *William Tell*'s gunners pounded the smaller British ship but still her flag flew.

Three hours after the battle had started, *Leander* was dead in the water – as dead as a hundred French sailors – and now Captain Berry lowered his flag and surrendered.

The British captain was rowed across to the French ship. His uniform was bloodstained and torn, his wig and hat twisted and burned. He took his sword from his belt and handed it to Admiral Villeneuve. 'We are your prisoners, sir.'

'Yes, Captain. You were foolish to even *try* to fight us.'

Captain Edward Berry shrugged, 'We were sure you French had no stomach for a fight.'

'Who said that?' Villeneuve snorted.

'It was Admiral Nelson, actually,' Berry sighed.

***

Meanwhile, on board Justice...

Mad Mac kept the pistol at the head of the French merchant captain while the sailors untied Jem and Meg Hawkwood. When they were in the rowing boat he called down, 'Bring the *Alerte* alongside! We'll take our fifty per cent!'

Meg rowed across to give the order to Grundle and Hope, Isaac and Jones.

An hour later fifteen barrels of wine and a dozen bales of woollen cloth were in *Alerte*'s hold. Captain Macdonald was back on board. 'Man the guns,' he ordered his crew.

'She isn't armed, Captain!' Meg argued. 'You can't sink an unarmed merchant. It's not fair. It's murder.'

Mac looked at her with his single savage eye. 'Mrs Hawkwood, I have just saved your life using good old-fashioned pirate tactics. There is nothing like a gun to the head to make a man see sense. A pirate that plays fair is a pirate blowing in the breeze with a rope around her neck ... and her son's neck.'

Meg bit her lip and lowered her eyes. She couldn't argue. Mac sniffed. 'If we leave *Justice* she'll sail straight into the French harbour in Malta and send a warship after us. We know *William Tell* is around these waters somewhere. So my plan isn't to sink *Justice*.'

'It isn't?'

'Of course not! I may be ruthless, but why would I sink a ship with half a cargo still on board? It would be a waste. No, I just want to stop her sailing.' He turned to the crew. 'Mister Grundle?'

'Yes, sir.'

'Any chain shot in the lockers?'

'Yes, sir.'

'Load the cannon with chain shot, aim at the French trader's masts and bring them down.'

'Yes, sir.'

Grundle and Hope, Isaac and Jones set about loading the cannon with chain shot.

Chain shot is small cannonballs chained together. But I bet you'd worked that out, hadn't you? See? You are more clever than you look, aren't you?

Meg stood at the starboard rail of *Alerte* and called across, 'Captain de Nantes! Clear your decks ... we're bringing down your masts and we don't want anyone to get hurt!'

'Yes we do!' Jem argued. 'Get *hurt*? They were going to hang us, Ma and throw us to the fishes. I wouldn't mind if the crew of *Justice* all ended up as mincemeat!'

Meg turned to her son and said, 'You're starting to sound like a pirate. Stop it. We are poor ... we want to make enough money to start a new life. But you can't build a new life on the corpses of helpless sailors.'

Jem went silent. He went below decks to prepare the powder for the guns.

Weasel-faced Isaac was the best gunner on the crew of *Alerte* and aimed the cannon at the main mast of *Justice*. The first blast sent the chained cannonballs spinning like a deadly top; they sliced through the rigging ropes and lost a lot of force. The next shot struck the mast and worked like a saw to cut through it. The mast creaked and fell. A second mast was brought down before Captain Macdonald called, 'Cease fire.'

The French sailors came back on deck to look at their ruined ship. Their captain looked close to tears. Meg turned to her son. 'He probably worked all his life to get a ship as fine as *Justice* and we wrecked it.'

'Serves him right for trying to kill us,' Jem said.

'Exactly,' Meg nodded. 'Which is why we need to be careful who we hurt. Someday something will happen that serves us right. Even wrecking that ship may cost us.'

'How, Ma?'

'I don't know ... you never know how justice will work.'

'Raise the sails and head west,' Captain Macdonald ordered and *Alerte* began to move slowly away from the French merchant ship.

'We're a bit slow, Captain,' Hope said.

'Of course we are, you gulpin. We've just added more weight to the ship. She's nearly full to the gunnels. She's bound to be slow. All we need now is a few bags of sugar.'

'To go with the tea?' Hope asked.

'No ... because sugar sells well in any port. We may meet a sugar ship on the way home.'

'Is that where we're headed?' Hope asked ... hopefully.

'I reckon,' his captain said.

'We're going home!' Hope cried and the grinning crew set about their work eagerly now.

'Home,' Meg Hawkwood said.

'Home,' Jem smiled.

FRENCH FRIED

Saturday 19 August 1798

The slightly shabby warship *William Tell* made its way slowly back to the French port at Malta. She was towing the even more broken *Leander* behind.

'Ship ahead!'

Admiral Villeneuve peered through his telescope. 'She's a merchant ship ... but looks as if she's been in a storm. We've not seen any storms in these waters for weeks. Strange. Ah! She is flying the French flag from what is left of her masts. Let's go and help.'

When *William Tell* reached the ship the Admiral saw she was named *Justice*. The crew brought the warship to a halt. Captain de Nantes from the *Justice* was rowed across. 'What happened, citizen?' Villeneuve asked.

'Pirates,' de Nantes spat.

'Pirates? No. The days of pirates are long gone. Were they Greek? Turkish? What were they sailing?'

'They were British, and they were sailing in a French sloop of war ... *Alerte*,' the merchant explained.

Admiral turned to the captain of *William Tell*. 'Bring the prisoner, Captain Berry, to me.'

As the Frenchmen shared a cup of wine, Captain Berry was led before them. 'Ah, Captain Berry. I hope my crew are treating you well?'

Edward Berry shrugged. 'I don't like French food.'

'You will have to get used to it. When we invade England and rule you, *then* you will get used to it.'

Berry gave the Admiral a warm smile. 'That will never happen. Never.'

Edward Berry must have forgotten his history lessons. It HAD happened once before. A bloke called William the Conqueror invaded from France in 1066 ... and won.

***

The *Alerte* ploughed through the sea like a wet dog. 'It will take us a month to get back to England at this rate,' Grundle moaned. 'We should throw some of the prizes overboard.'

'I don't like a crewman that complains,' Captain Macdonald said. 'Did I ever tell you the tale of the pirate, Ned Low?'

'No, Captain,' Grundle said. 'Gather round, crew!' the sailor called. 'The captain's going to tell us one of his tall tales.'

When they were seated on the deck Mad Mac fixed them with his eye, one at a time. 'Ned Low was a pickpocket in America...'

'I thought he was a pirate,' Isaac argued in his weasely way.

'Whose story is this? Avast yer nizzie. He was a pickpocket that *turned* to the pirate trade. He was the cruellest man I ever sailed with...'

'I thought Black Bart was the cruellest man you ever sailed with,' Jem put in.

'Do you want to hear my tale or do you not?'

'Sorry, Captain.'

'Ned Low was a pickpocket who turned to piracy. He stopped ships and kidnapped the crews. He forced them to sail with him,' Mac explained.

'That's not cruel,' Jem said.

'Low refused to have married men on his ship ... he was always worried they'd run off home to their wives. So if he captured a married man he shot him in the head!'

'*That's* cruel,' Jem admitted.

'Low once captured the Spanish galleon *Moncova* and he killed every one of the 50 prisoners with his cutlass,' Mac went on.

'That must have made his arm ache!' Hope cried.

'He was a strong man. That wasn't the cruellest thing though ... he killed one Spanish sailor, cut out his heart, and made the sailor's best friend eat it.'

'Nasty.'

'As for the cook – he was French. Low told him he was so greasy he would fry well ... and he had him burned alive.'

'And did Low get away with it?' Meg asked. 'You tell these tales of cruel pirates but you never say what happened to them, do you?'

'The French cook was a mistake,' Mac said. 'Ned Low was captured by the French navy. Of course they didn't show him any mercy and they hanged him.'

'Better than being burned alive, I suppose,' Jones put in.

The stories of Ned Low are true ... but he died around the year 1724 – that's 74 years before our tale began. It would make Captain Macdonald over 120 at the time of the story. Oh, dear, what a liar. An even bigger liar than you, when you tell teacher, 'Please, Miss, the dog ate my homework!'

'Best of all is not to get caught and punished,' Jem said wisely and the crew nodded.

'We are not *going* to get caught,' Captain Macdonald sniffed.

***

On board William Tell...

Admiral Villeneuve looked out over the waters of the Mediterranean. He looked to the west where the *Alerte* had sailed off with its French wine on board.

'Tell me, Captain Berry, what happened to our sloop of war, *Alerte*? You captured her when you were lucky enough to win the battle at Abukir Bay.'

'We sent her back to England as a prize,' Berry said.

The admiral waved a hand towards the French captain beside him. 'This is Captain de Nantes of that ruined French merchant ship you see alongside. He says he was robbed and wrecked by pirates from the *Alerte*.'

Berry could only shake his head in wonder. 'I ... I can only guess the crew were engaged in an act of war. The merchant ship is French.'

Villeneuve looked angry. 'It was *piracy*, Captain Berry. She did not attempt to sink *Justice* or capture her crew. Just *rob* her. Let me tell you, once we have left *Leander* in Malta and seen Captain de Nantes safe ashore, we will search the Mediterranean Sea and find this pirate. We will blow him into so many pieces even the smallest fish will have bits of his flesh to feed on.'

***

Monday 21 August 1798

Admiral Nelson scratched his head where it itched under the bandage. It had been a day full of problems. He needed a rest. But every time he sat down in his cabin there was a knock at the door. 'Sorry to disturb you, Admiral, but this is urgent...'

The first visit of the day had been a messenger from a British merchant ship, *Clover*. 'Sorry to disturb you, Admiral,' the seaman said. He had a face as round as a saucer and red as a roasted lobster.

'That's quite all right. I was awake anyway. And my captain said it was urgent.'

'Yes, sir, we thought you really ought to know. And I said to my crew, I think Lord Nelson ought to know and they said that you probably already knew and I said...'

'Yes!' Nelson said loudly. 'Just tell me what it is.'

'Well,' the lobster face said, 'we were sailing past Malta and one of the crew cried, 'French warship ahead!' I nearly wet myself! I mean we only have one cannon on the whole ship and that *William Tell* had sixty!'

'Eighty,' Nelson said quietly. 'Did she attack you?'

'No, sir! She couldn't. She was too busy towing another ship. And I said to my crew, I think Lord Nelson ought to know, and they said that you probably already knew, and I said...'

'Get on with it!' Nelson ordered.

'Sorry, Lord Nelson...'

'I have not been made a Lord ... yet,' the little admiral snapped.

'Sorry, your lordship ... I mean ... sorry, *sir* ... but would you believe it? What was the ship *William Tell* had in tow?'

'I don't know,' Nelson said. His teeth were tight together and it was making his head ache. 'I thought that's what you'd come to tell me!'

'Yes, your lordship, sir. It was *Leander*, sir. When I was last docked in Portsmouth I remember seeing her there and...'

'*Leander*!' Nelson cried. 'The French have taken her?'

'Yes, your lordship, sir.'

'Get out!'

'What?'

'Out!'

'And I said to my crew, I think Lord Nelson might offer a reward for that information I said...'

'Out before I have you pushed down the muzzle of a cannon and fired off my ship. Out! I need to make plans.'

'Yes, your lordship, sir ... oh, there's no need to draw your sword...'

And the man was gone.

Moments later there was a rap on the door. 'Enter!' Nelson said and a young officer entered. 'Sorry, Admiral, was that man a nuisance?'

'No, but his news was. *Leander* has been captured. We need to send another ship back to London with our reports. Which is the next ship to leave the line?'

'*Goliath*, sir.'

'Get her ready to leave as soon as the copies of our report are ready. Tell Captain Foley to leave as soon as his ship is loaded with food and water.'

'Sorry, sir, Captain Foley has a fever. He is too sick to command his ship. He's being cared for on board *Vanguard*.'

'Then Lieutenant Darke is in command. Tell him he sails for England this afternoon,' Nelson snapped.

'Yes, sir.'

The admiral sat at his table and buried his aching head in his hands. There was a knock at the door. 'What?' he screamed.

'There is a Captain Samuel Swift on the ship,' an officer said.

'Swift? We don't have a Captain Swift in the fleet.'

'No, sir. He's from a merchant ship *Peachy Face*.'

'*Peachy* what?'

'*Face*, sir. I wouldn't bother you. But he was babbling some strange tale. He says a Navy ship stopped him and took a tax ... ten per cent of his cargo. He said it was to pay for the war against France. He decided to return to get some Egyptian cotton to fill up the space on his ship. But no one in port had heard of this new tax. He called to check with us that this tax was what you ordered.'

'That is utter nonsense,' Nelson moaned. 'It sounds as if he has been tricked. It's nothing to do with me.'

'I know, sir,' the young man said, 'it's just ... the ship that stopped him ... well ... it was the ship you sent home as a prize. The *Alerte*.'

Admiral Nelson closed his eyes.

I know, I know, don't tell me. Nelson only had one eye. But I can't say 'He closed his eye,' can I? Both of his eyelids went down when he closed his eye ... so he closed his eyes. Or, if you want to be really fussy I could say, 'He closed his eyelids.' But that's just as silly ... at least that's what eye think.

'*Alerte*? The ship we sent under the command of who?'

'Seaman Macdonald. A one-eyed rogue if ever there was one,' the officer said grimly.

'There is nothing wrong with having one eye,' Nelson said furiously.

'Oh! No, sir ... sorry, sir! But Seaman Macdonald was always telling pirate tales to the crew. It sounds as if he's trying to live the pirate life.'

The admiral shook his head wearily. 'This tax idea is clever. The crew are stopping merchant ships and asking them for a sort of tax? Well, it's a new sort of piracy I suppose. But it's piracy all the same. He could have got away with it. It's too clever for Macdonald. There was a woman with him on the ship, wasn't there?'

'Yes, sir.'

'Then they can all hang on the same gallows.'

'Will you see Captain Swift of *Peachy Face*, Admiral?'

'No. Just thank him and tell him we will deal with it. Then tell Lieutenant Darke to set off for England at once. He can ask for news of *Alerte* at Gibraltar on the way. If he captures *Alerte*, he can throw the crew in chains, have them flogged and take them back to England to hang. If they put up a fight he can blow them out of the water.'

'Yes, sir. Anything else, sir?'

'Just let me rest. If anyone knocks on this door in the next hour I will shoot them.'

***

'Gather round, chaps!' Lieutenant Darke cried from the poop deck of *Goliath*. 'We sail with the tide!'

The crew of the *Goliath* didn't cheer as he expected. Master Gunner White said, 'Excuse me, sir...'

'We sail on a great mission,' Darke cried. 'To take our

mighty warship home to a heroes' welcome ... and to wipe out the last pirates on the seas.'

Still the crew looked worried.

'Excuse me sir, but about the tide...' Gunner White said.

'We sail as soon as it is high!' Darke said and smiled his chinless smile.

'This is the Mediterranean Sea, Mr Darke ... there are no tides in the Mediterranean Sea.'

'Eh? Ah! Yes ... I *knew* that,' Darke said. 'It's a sailing term ... I don't mean we sail with the *tide* ... which isn't there, of course. I mean we sail ... as soon as we are ready. Hoist the mainsail!'

'Excuse me, sir...'

'Yes, Midshipman?'

'We need a pilot boat to tow us clear of the fleet. If we raise the main sail now, the wind would drive us into Admiral Nelson's ship. He wouldn't be very pleased, Mr Darke.'

'Yes ... well, I knew that. I meant hitch us up to a pilot boat and then hoist the mainsail.'

'God help us all,' Gunner White moaned softly.

'And when we find Macdonald and his villains we will show them no mercy. I have wanted my revenge on that man for a long time and I will have it! I will have it! He has been giving me trouble since we left England. Laughing at me behind my back. Well now he'll find he who lasts laughs, laughs lastest. Let's away. Hoist the main ... er ... let's get underway. For King and country, death or glory! No pirate shall escape the justice of our noble crew. We shall blast them from the seas and hang them in chains for all the world to see. My blood boils at the name of Macdonald!'

'Jem is on that ship,' a young girl, a powder monkey, said quietly.

The master gunner turned to her and said, 'With Mr Darke in charge I think your friend Jem is safe.'

MUTINY AND MAROONING

Saturday 25 August 1798

A*lerte* battled on against the south-westerly wind. She rolled like a fully fed whale. The skies were greyer now they were nearing the Atlantic. The wind was cooler too. But the crew were restless.

They had found a sugar ship and now the holds of *Alerte* were crammed. She was heavy and low in the water. When the sea turned a little rough they were soaked on deck. Jem had to pile up sugar bags against the powder room door to stop water turning the gunpowder to wet gloop.

'How much further to Gibraltar now?' Grundle sighed.

Captain Macdonald was in one of his worst moods. 'The charts we took off *Justice* say it's half a day's sailing away. Then we turn north and we'll have the wind in our favour. We'll fly home like an albatross.'

'Who's Albert Ross? Jem asked. 'A pirate?'

'An *albatross* is a huge sea bird. It stays in the air for a year. Anyway, Grundle, if you want to see the Rock of Gibraltar earlier I can always pluck out one of your eyes and throw it ahead. Want me to do that, Grundle?'

'No, Captain.'

'No! Always remember what a kind captain I am. Not like Roche Brasiliano!'

'I suppose you sailed with him, did you?' Jem asked.

'Don't be stupid, lad. Roche died a hundred years ago.'

Meg smiled and said quietly, 'Most of the men he says he sailed with have been dead that long but it doesn't seem to stop him telling his tales!'

'So what did Roche do?' Jones asked. 'Something horrible?'

'I'm glad you asked me that, Jones. Roche was Dutch and they were at war with France. His favourite trick was to capture French sailors, tie them to a pole and roast them over a fire. If I met a French ship now that's what I'd do too.'

'An *unarmed* French ship,' Jem said. 'You only fight French ships like *Justice* that have no guns.'

Mad Mac leapt to his feet and drew his sword. 'I'll fight *any* Frenchman. It's like my friend Admiral Nelson says, "My blood boils at the name of a Frenchman!" One of my crew is worth twenty French sailors – no, *fifty*. Show me a French warship and I'll show you a sunken ship.'

'Even a ship as large as *William Tell*?' Jem asked.

'*William Tell*? Hah! I'd sink her easy as a paper ship on a village pond. Then I'd rip out the hearts of the French crew and eat them raw, just like Francoise l'Olonoise – a French pirate – used to do to our British lads. Raw! I'll eat them raw.'

Jem nodded. 'Then I hope you are hungry,' he said. '*William Tell* is just a league away from us. You can eat a hundred French hearts!'

'*What?*' Captain Macdonald leapt to the rigging and

looked over the stern of *Alerte*. His eye was wide as a saucer of milk and his skin as white. 'God's truth! Why didn't you tell me?' he screamed at the crew. 'Cram on every inch of sail, lads! Hurry! If we go as fast as we can then we may reach Gibraltar – there's a British naval base there ... they'll sail out and fight for us... *William Tell* won't dare face the British Navy alone. She ran away at Abukir Bay so she'll run away now.'

Grundle and Hope, Isaac and Jones hurried to obey. Jem frowned. 'I thought you *wanted* to fight the French. Eat their hearts raw.'

'Yes, well that was *before*. I'm not hungry *now*, am I?' Captain Macdonald whined.

That sounds reasonable. YOU wouldn't want to eat a raw human heart unless you were peckish, would you? To eat one just after you've stuffed yourself with a burger would be plain greedy.

Meg held her son by the shoulder. 'Jem, get down to the powder room and start bringing powder up to the guns. We need Isaac and Jones on the guns – I'll work the sails with Grundle and Captain Macdonald can steer. We'll only have two cannon working but it's better than none.'

'You think *William Tell* will catch us?'

'Oh, yes,' Meg said. She turned to Mac as he struggled to raise a mizzen sail. 'Sorry, Captain, but there's only one way we'll reach Gibraltar in time ... and that's if we throw the sacks of sugar and tea and the bales of silk overboard

'... all the heavy stuff.'

'My treasure!' he wailed.

'Your treasure won't be any use to you if it's at the bottom of the Mediterranean, and us with it. Give the order, Captain.'

'A mutiny is it?' he raged. 'Trying to give your captain orders are you? You know what Blackbeard did to pirates that mutinied against him?'

'Cut their toenails short and ate the clippings?' Meg smiled.

'He put them ashore on a desert island... He left them with a barrel of water and a pistol. We pirates called it being marooned. And the pistol wasn't to hunt with. It was to blow out their own brains when they were starving and being eaten alive by insects! Would you like me to do that to you, Meg Hawkwood?'

She threw back her red hair and laughed. 'Die a certain death under the French guns or take my chance on a desert island? Ooooh! Hard choice, Captain. Put me and Jem ashore at the next desert island. Where is it?'

Mad Mac stamped his foot and said, 'You know there are no desert islands for a thousand miles!'

'Oh, dear, then you can't maroon us! But I sailed with one of the greatest women pirates ever ... Anne Bonney!'

You've guessed it. Anne Bonney died in 1722 ... far too long ago for Meg to have met her. But Meg reckoned if Mad Mac could lie then so could she! Fair's fair ... as the man on the roundabouts used to say.

'I've heard of her!' Captain Macdonald said. 'She was pirate Jack Rackham's girlfriend. When she got fed up with him she was happy to watch him hang!'

Meg sighed. 'Yes. And she was tender-hearted as a robin compared to me. Now Anne Bonney told me there is an interesting pirate's law... In a battle the crew must obey the captain ... whatever he orders.'

'That's true! If you don't, I'll gut you and eat your liver!' the captain laughed.

'Ah, BUT,' she said, raising a finger. 'When the ship isn't in a battle then the crew choose the captain. They can sack the old captain and pick a new one.'

'I never heard that pirate law,' Mac said.

'I have,' Grundle said as he hauled on a rope to raise the mizzen staysail.

Meg's grin was as wide as the fore topsail spar. 'Lads!' she cried to the crew. 'It's time to choose a captain.'

They gathered in a circle on the main deck and listened. 'Does anyone have any ideas about who should be captain?'

'Captain Macdonald is captain,' Jones said.

'Hah!' Mac cried. 'That's one vote for me.'

'I think my ma should be captain,' Jem said.

'One vote each,' Meg said.

'I vote for me,' Mac cackled. 'Two-one.'

'And I vote for me,' Meg told him '... two-two.'

They turned towards Isaac, Hope and Grundle.

'Captain Macdonald is a hero ... he says he's sailed with all the great pirates,' Grundle argued. 'I vote for him.'

'Ah, but look at the mess we're in now!' ferret-faced

Isaac hissed. 'Meg Hawkwood gets my vote. Three-all.'

Everyone turned to Hope. His pudding face was set in a frown. 'What?' he asked.

'Who do you want as captain?' Jem asked. 'Mad Mac or Ma?'

'Well ... Mad Mac IS the captain ... why do we need to change?' Hope asked.

Isaac looked at Jones and Jones looked at Isaac. 'That's a *really* good question, Hope. Shows your brains haven't been blown out with gunpowder.'

'Thanks, Jones!'

'Why do we need to change?' Meg put in. 'Because Captain Macdonald wants us to wallow along till *William Tell* catches us and sinks us. But if you make ME captain I'd throw all our loot overboard, speed up and get to Gibraltar harbour before the Frenchies reach us.'

'Hmmm!' Hope nodded. 'A hard choice.'

'Vote for Ma,' Jem cried.

'Ma?' Hope said. 'I had a ma. And do you know what she said?'

'She probably said, "Bring me some ale from the tavern or I'll smack you round the ear," ... that's what my ma always said,' Isaac sighed.

'No,' Hope said. 'Ma always said that a change is as good as a rest ... so I think MY ma would want a change. She's vote for Meg Hawkwood ... and so do I.'

'I'll feed you to the sharks, you sea rat!' Mad Mac roared and drew his cutlass.

'Sorry!' Meg said, gripping his wrist in her powerful hand. 'But you can't do that. You're not the captain any longer. I say we need every hand on deck to save ourselves.' She turned to Grundle and Hope, Isaac and Jones. 'Let's empty everything over the side as quick as you can ... and that includes you, young Jem Hawkwood ... and YOU ... ordinary seaman Macdonald, get to work.'

The crew sighed and all but wept to see their treasure drift away. But orders are orders.

Meg herself took the rudder and steered the ship as well as she could. Over the stern she could see *William Tell* drawing nearer.

The crew kept throwing their loot over the side. They sailed on and left behind a trail of their treasure.

On the poop deck of *William Tell*, Admiral Villeneuve looked through his telescope and smiled. 'They are wasting their time. They will never make it.'

'Shall we man the guns ready to sink her?' Captain Fontaine asked.

'No, Captain,' Villeneuve said. 'During the Revolution I was in the south of the country while the nobles were being executed. The citizens there started to massacre them by the dozen. But they decided the guillotine was too slow. So the executioners chained prisoners together, put them in barges, towed them into the middle of the River Loire and sank them. Still today sailing ships pull up anchors there with rotting skeletons hooked on them.'

'Yes, sir?' the captain said, unsure of what his commander wanted.

'That is what I want for those English pirates. I want them fastened in chains. I want them put into a rowing boat. And then I want our gunners to have a little fun ... there will be a prize to see who can be the first to hit the rowing boat and drown them.'

'You think they will give up without a fight then?' Captain Fontaine asked.

'Of course ... if we promise to spare their lives.'

'Oh, sir! You'd lie to them. What about the honour of a Frenchman's word.'

Villeneuve bared his teeth in anger. 'Honour? Pirates do not know the meaning of the word.'

***

With every bag and box thrown over the side, the *Alerte* seemed to leap up and speed forward. Grundle and Hope, Isaac and Jones worked happily.

Mad Mac climbed the mast and looked back. '*William Tell* has stopped gaining on us!' he cried, excited as a boy with a football. He turned to look over the bows. 'Coastline ahead ... a high rock. I think it must be Gibraltar!'

'We're going to make it, Ma!' Jem cried.

'Call me Captain Hawkwood, Jem lad, or I'll give you fifty lashes you scurvy lubber!' she said.

'Yes ... Ma,' Jem smiled.

***

The lookout on the top of Gibraltar Rock raced down a stone stairway to the Navy office on the quayside. He ran across to the commander's room, knocked on the door and burst in as soon as the commander said, 'Enter.'

Sir ... French sloop of war flying a British flag ... on her way here from the East.'

'That must be *Alerte*,' the commander said.

'She's being chased by a French battleship, sir – eighty guns by the look of her. *Alerte* is sunk if we don't get help to her!'

'How far away?'

'Less than a league, sir. She'll catch her in half an hour.'

'We can't get any ships ready for sea in half an hour!' the commander groaned. 'Most of the crews are ashore anyway!'

'There's a warship just arrived from Egypt ... she's got

a full crew and most of her seventy-four guns still in action.'

'What's her name?'

'*Goliath*, sir.'

'Ah, tell Captain Foley to sail out immediately to the assistance of *Alerte*.'

'Captain Foley isn't in command, sir.'

'Tell the chap in command then. What's his name?'

'Darke, sir. Lieutenant Jacob Darke.'

'Send Lieutenant Darke to rescue the poor fellows on *Alerte*.'

BARREL AND BOASTS

On board Goliath...

Lieutenant Darke gathered his crew on the deck. 'Right, chaps! We have been ordered to go straight back out of port to attack a French battleship of the line ... it must one that escaped the Battle of the Nile. There is also a French sloop of war out there ... probably the pirate we have been hunting since we left Egypt. First we sink the Frenchie ... and then we sink the pirate.'

'Sorry, sir, but shouldn't we be trying to capture them? I mean the prize money would be marvellous,' Master Gunner White said.

'Oh, all right. First we *capture* the Frenchie and then we smash Seaman Macdonald's ship into firewood! I want to see him blown into even smaller pieces! I want to see him hanged in chains! I want to see him grovel for his life!'

'Excuse me, sir, but shouldn't we be setting sail? We can't risk the French ship trapping us in the harbour. We need to be on the open seas ... and we'll have the wind behind us, the way Admiral Nelson likes to fight.'

'Yes!' Darke cried. 'To battle! I could be the new Nelson! Up anchor. Man the guns. Clear the decks! We must hate the French like we hate the devil!'

The fresh south-westerly breeze carried *Goliath* out into the Mediterranean Sea.

On *William Tell* Admiral Villeneuve watched *Goliath* slide out of Gibraltar harbour. 'One of their damaged ships,' he told his captain. 'She won't have all of her 74 guns.'

Captain Fontaine looked worried. 'We don't have all of our 80 guns, sir. The larboard side took a fearful battering from *Leander* at Malta.'

Villeneuve looked annoyed. 'Then make sure we hit them with broadsides from our starboard guns.'

The captain coughed into his hand. 'They do have the wind behind them...'

'So?'

'So they can decide which side to attack,' the captain pointed out.

'Turn our ship to show them our starboard – their captain will attack the side we want him to!'

The French captain muttered, 'Only if he's an idiot.'

***

Captain Meg Hawkwood of *Alerte* saw *Goliath* sail towards them. 'She'll deal with the French for us,' she sighed heavily. 'We're safe.'

Jem was looking through the telescope. 'It's Lieutenant Darke on the poop deck … Captain Ma … he's an idiot! The French will sink him and come after us. The French ship is bigger… If she wins we lose … and remember how damaged *Goliath* was at Abukir Bay?'

'Or *he'll* sink the French then come after us … either way we lose,' Mad Mac said. 'He hates me. If *he* wins, *we* lose. We all hang as pirates.'

Meg closed her eyes.

'We sailed *Goliath* from England – we beat the French at Abukir Bay. We've a lot of friends on board her. If we let Lieutenant Darke die, then our old friends die too.'

'What do you mean "let" them die'?' weasel Isaac asked. 'We can't do anything about it.'

Mad Mac said, 'Yes we could… If I were captain I'd go and fight *William Tell*.'

'Hah!' Jones gasped. 'A twelve-gun sloop of war against an eighty-gun battleship? There's no way we could win.'

'Remember Abukir Bay,' Jem said quietly. 'A ship can fight to the starboard side or the larboard … but a ship that tries to fight both sides at once has problems. If we make the gunners and powder monkeys run to fire at us then there are less to fire at *Goliath*.' He reminded them.

Meg nodded slowly. 'I agree with Mac. We turn. We fight.'

'We die,' Jones grumbled … but hurried off to help turn *Alerte* around.

***

Lieutenant Darke's watery eyes shone. 'See! The Frenchie is showing us her starboard side ... let's attack it. Prepare the starboard guns.'

Master Gunner White waited a moment. 'Maybe that's what their captain wants, sir ... maybe she is weak on the larboard side?'

Darke's little chin vanished into his chubby neck and he pulled his head back in disgust. 'I am commander. I decide. You do as you are told or you will get fifty lashes!' he screamed.

'Will that be before or after the battle ... sir?' White sniffed and walked away to get his gunners and powder monkeys ready.

'Full sail!' Darke ordered. 'Nelson himself would be proud of us, chaps!'

***

Admiral Villeneuve and his captain watched in wonder as *Goliath* raced towards them. 'I said that only a fool would attack our starboard side. This is a great day for the Revolution, Captain. The day a French battleship smashes one of Nelson's ships and sails free from the Mediterranean. Imagine the damage we can do when we reach the Atlantic. We will be heroes. Are our starboard guns ready?'

'Yes, Admiral. We have twenty filled with chain shot to wreck her rigging and a dozen with grapeshot to cut her crew down.'

Grapeshot wasn't firing grapes and killing the enemy with a blast of wine. Grapeshot was a cannon packed with small bullets the size of grapes ... it was like being shot at with a hundred muskets. Deadly if you didn't duck. Warships used it against enemy ships. Napoleon Bonaparte used it against his own poor people in Paris to keep them in order. Blood and flesh spattered the walls of the city. Nice man.

'Ship to larboard,' the lookout cried from the forecastle in the bows of *William Tell*.

'Hah!' Villeneuve snorted. 'It's not just the British that have idiots on their ship.' The admiral marched down the main deck and shouted at the lookout, 'Don't you know your starboard from your larboard? The British ship is on the *starboard* side!'

130

The lookout glared at him. 'I know! I *know*! But there's a ship on the larboard side *as well*. I'm not stupid ... sir.' If the lookout had dared he would have stuck out his tongue at his admiral.

Villeneuve hurried back to the poop deck for his telescope and put it to his eye. He lowered it slowly. 'Captain ... that pirate we were chasing ... he has turned around and is heading towards us! I think he is planning to attack!'

Captain Fontaine looked across the wind-whipped waves and his mouth fell open. 'He's attacking to larboard. She only has six guns on that side but she can still do a lot of damage. I'll send some gunners across to defend her.'

'A dozen guns should do it.'

'I'm not sure we have a dozen guns left ... *Leander* gave the larboard gun-ports a fearful battering, sir.'

Villeneuve shook his head. 'Not one idiot British captain but two!'

***

Jem raced up and down the steep stairways to bring powder for each of the six guns. They only had three gunners ... Grundle, Isaac and Jones ... while Meg steered and Hope and Mad Mac sailed the sloop. But the gunners could fire two cannon each and could possibly even have time to reload before they swept past the French ship.

'Black Bart fought bigger Spanish galleons than that with a smaller pirate ship than this,' Mac cried. 'The trick is to take our ship in close as we can. Their cannon will be firing over our heads!'

Meg nodded and steered the *Alerte* towards the *William Tell*. Cannon roared from the French ship as she fired her starboard guns at *Goliath*. The British warship shuddered and rigging fell but the wind drove her on and when she was closer, Master Gunner White gave the order to fire.

William Tell was hurt by the gunfire and Villeneuve looked in horror at the broken and bleeding sailors slumped on his deck as *Goliath* raced past and began to turn for a second run.

'Throw the dead over the side – sand the decks so you don't slip in their blood. Get the carpenters to patch that rail before someone falls overboard!' he yelled.

At that moment the guns on the larboard side fired and the warship shook as the little sloop fired back.

The shots from the *William Tell* sailed high over the *Alerte*'s decks and Meg Hawkwood's crew were unhurt, but her topsails were shredded and fluttering like paper kites. Meg turned *Alerte* hard until the ship crunched up against the side of *William Tell*.

The wind carried *Alerte* away and past the stern of the French ship. But now there were just six crew aboard her. One man was missing.

***

Admiral Villeneuve stood at the cracked rail of the poop deck and called down, 'Tell Captain Fontaine to fill the cannon with heavy shot. This time we'll sink the little British pest.'

A blood-soaked master gunner looked up. 'Sorry, sir, the captain's dead.'

'Then YOU do it!' Villeneuve roared. 'The British are turning! They will attack again. What are you waiting for?'

'I'm waiting for you to tell us what to do,' the gunner said.

'I have already *told* you what to do!' the admiral raged.

'Yes, sir, but that was before...' and the gunner nodded to the poop deck.

'Before what?'

'Before I had this cutlass ready to slice off your foolish French head,' a voice said from behind the admiral.

Villeneuve turned around slowly and found himself face to face with a one-eyed man. The man held a rusty old cutlass in his hand and it was at the neck of the French commander.

'Take out your sword and hand it to me – hilt first – and tell your crew to stop firing. Then haul down your filthy French flag.'

Villeneuve tried to smile. 'My friend, we have enough cannon to blow your ships out of the water three times over.'

'I served with Blackbeard, you know. He taught me how to split a man from the top of his head down to his belly. That's what I'll do to you if you don't hand over your sword. Your captain is dead. You will be dead. The crew can't fight without a leader. Surrender or die.'

Villeneuve gave a great sigh. He slowly took his sword from its sheath, held it by the blade and passed it to Mad Mac. He turned back to the master gunner on the deck. 'Cease firing. Tell the midshipman to take down the flag.'

'Yes, sir,' the gunner nodded and hurried off to obey.

The admiral turned to the one-eyed seaman. 'Sir ... this is a great disgrace for me. To lose my ship – a ship of the French Revolution – to a common pirate. Will you allow me one favour?'

'What's that, matey?' Mac asked.

'Allow me to surrender my sword to a proper British warship ... look, she is headed this way now.'

Mad Mac watched as *Goliath* drew close to *William Tell* and began to get her crew ready to board her. As soon as Darke saw him he'd be arrested. He shrugged. 'Why not, eh? And you will do one thing for me, in return?'

'What's that?'

'You say I jumped on board your ship but you shot me with your pistols and I fell into the sea, dead.'

Villeneuve smiled sadly. 'Ah, a pirate has no friends, eh?'

Mac stared at the admiral with his one eye glinting. 'I have some very good friends,' he said. 'And they'll be wondering where I am. Good day, Admiral ... *bon chance* as my friend Francoise l'Olonoise used to say.'

***

Lieutenant Darke put a British crew on board the *William Tell* and ordered her to sail into Gibraltar harbour. 'See?' he told Master Gunner White. 'Nelson could not have done better.'

'No, sir. Remarkable.'

'You wanted me to attack the larboard side, but I knew better.'

'You did, sir. Of course *Alerte* attacked their larboard

and that helped a lot. You may not have won without the help of the pirate.'

Darke's round and foolish face turned furious. 'Nonsense, White. Nonsense. The pirate was trying to save his own skin ... Macdonald probably sailed towards *William Tell* to surrender. He saw me coming and knew I'd sink him as soon as I'd dealt with the Frenchie.'

'If you say so, sir. We're alongside *Alerte* now, sir. You're going to let him go, aren't you? His crew used to be part of this crew. Meg and her Jem were very popular. Even Macdonald had a lot of friends on our ship.'

'All the more to enjoy the hanging. Rig up a noose from the top mast, White.'

The old gunner turned and walked away without a word.

Lieutenant Darke walked to the side rail and climbed down into the sloop below. Meg and Jem, Grundle and Hope, Isaac and Jones watched in silence. 'I am arresting you for piracy and sentence you to hang.'

'We're not pirates, sir,' Meg said quietly. 'We are just taking *Alerte* back to England ... as Captain Foley ordered.'

'You have robbed British ships on the way,' Darke said.

'Robbed what, sir?' Meg asked, wide-eyed.

'Silk cloth, boxes of tea and spices!'

Meg looked at the crew. Grundle and Hope, Isaac and Jones shook their heads in amazement. Isaac stuck his ferret face forward. 'Oh, sir, if you find one scrap of silk or one leaf of tea on this ship you can hang us all ... in fact I'll hang myself! Captain Hawkwood here is as honest as the day is long.'

'*Captain* Hawkwood? So it's true what that Frenchman said about the villain Macdonald being shot dead?'

'We all watched him fall into the sea... He had so many bullets in him the sea turned red!' Jem said.

'Shame,' Darke snapped. 'I will search your ship anyway ... remember ... one scrap of silk and you all hang!'

He marched along the decks, peered into the holds and the cabins. Then he saw the barrel on the deck. 'Wine?' he asked. 'That wasn't on *Alerte* when she left Egypt. You stole it!'

Meg turned a tap on the bottom of the barrel. 'Fresh water, sir. We have to have fresh water.'

Darke's small mouth was pinched tight. At last he said, 'Get this ship back to Portsmouth as soon as you can.'

'Yes, Captain Darke,' Meg said with a small curtsey.

'Captain? Ah! Yes. Sadly I'm just a lieutenant at the moment,' Darke said and his face turned a little pink. 'Captain Darke sounds good, don't you think?'

'But we'll be calling you *Admiral* Darke before this war is over,' Jem cried.

'Oh, nonsense, nonsense ... oh, perhaps ... yes, probably. Right. Carry on you chaps. Safe journey.'

Meg, Jem, Grundle and Hope, Isaac and Jones called back, 'Thank you, Admiral Darke!'

*****

By evening *Alerte* was in the Atlantic Ocean and heading north to Britain. The crew gathered on the deck to sample some of Meg Hawkwood's best stewed beef and cabbage and fresh-baked bread. Even as captain she cooked for the crew.

'Poor old Mac,' Grundle sighed. 'Missing this meal. I'll bet pirates back in Blackbeard's day never ate this well.'

'He wasn't a pirate,' Jones said suddenly.

'What?' Jem cried. 'He sailed with all the greatest pirates ever to roam the seven seas.'

'No he didn't. He was a pot man in a tavern in Dover. He served ale and listened to the old tales of the sailors. In the end he started telling the tales himself ... as if he'd been there!'

'So how did he end up on a British warship?' Jem asked.

'Same as the rest of us. The press gang came around. We all tried to argue we weren't sailors ... but mad old Mac was *boasting* about sailing the world! Of course they took him too!'

'He said he lost his eye in a pirate battle,' Jem said.

'He lost his eye when he fell down stairs drunk one night. He'd never set foot on a ship before they pressed him.'

'Poor Mac.'

The crew picked stew from their teeth with a slurping louder than the slap of waves. At last Jem spoke.

'But, when it came to attacking *William Tell* he acted

just like a pirate, didn't he?' the boy asked. 'I mean, Nelson and his Navy warships fight with guns, but pirates climb aboard the enemy and fight hand to hand. In the end he was a *real* hero and a *real* pirate.'

'I vote Mad Mac be restored to the post of captain of this ship ... till we get to Portsmouth,' Meg said. 'All those in favour, raise a hand?'

Six hands went up.

Jem chewed on a delicious piece of beef that had been stuck between his teeth. 'Ma?'

'Yes, son?'

'Do you think we ought to let Captain Macdonald out of the water barrel now? Lieutenant Darke's been gone for three hours.'

Meg Hawkwood sighed. 'I suppose so. It's been so peaceful without him.'

Grundle trundled over to the water barrel, pulled out the nails and lifted off the lid.

Mac climbed out wearily. 'There was still water in that barrel, you know!' he said.

'We'll never be able to drink it now,' Jem told him.

'Yes ... no, but my feet have been in the water for hours!'

'I've never seen them so clean, Captain,' Meg smiled.

'Who are you calling *captain*? You're captain,' he said.

'Not any more. The crew think you were such a great hero you should

138

captain us all the way back to Portsmouth. *And* claim two shares of the prize money!'

Mad Mac's single eye went blind with tears. 'Oh,' he said.

'I know it's not as much as the treasure we threw overboard, but I'll be able to set up in a tavern,' Meg said.

'If you need a pot man then I'm a good ... er ... learner. I could *learn* to be a pot man!'

'So you've given up the pirate life, have you?' Meg asked gently.

'It's not the same as it used to be,' Mad Mac sighed. 'Not like the old days when Spanish galleons sailed the seas, packed with treasure chests of gold and silver, pieces of eight and doubloons, diamonds as bright as the moon and emeralds as green as the sea.'

'The pirate days are over, then,' Jem nodded.

'They are. Those are the exact words Black Bart used to say when I sailed the seven seas with him!'

The crew looked at one another wearily. 'Grundle?' Meg said.

'Yes, Meg?'

'Would you like to pop Captain Macdonald back in the water barrel till we get to Portsmouth?'

'What?' Mac gasped with a one-eyed blink. 'What did I *say*?' the last pirate cried.

EPILOGUE – TERRIBLE TRUTHS

On 1 August 1798 Admiral Nelson's British Navy caught General Napoleon's fleet at Abukir Bay off the mouth of the Nile. *Goliath* led the way behind the line of French ships and took them by surprise.

Women helped out on the fighting ships in those days – in 2000 the grave of a British woman sailor was found at Abukir along with a couple of tiny children who died in the battle.

Napoleon's fleet was destroyed ... except for *William Tell*, which escaped along with Admiral Villeneuve. Napoleon slipped out of Egypt, returned to France and became the emperor. Villeneuve was captured soon afterwards when the British took the island of Malta, but he was soon set free.

Leander was attacked on her way back to Britain by one of the French battleships that had escaped at Abukir Bay. After a fierce battle she was forced to surrender.

The mighty French ship *Orient* blew up and killed most of her crew. A story said that *Orient*'s Captain Casabianca was killed. His son stood on the deck and refused to leave his post till he had an order from his father – the order never came. The 12-year-old boy was blown up with the ship.

Then, thirty years after the battle, a poet wrote a poem called 'Casabianca' and it became one of the most popular poems ever written...

'The boy stood on the burning deck
Whence all but he had fled;
The flame that lit the battle's wreck
Shone round him o'er the dead.'

Nelson died seven years after his victory at Abukir Bay. He was shot at the Battle of Trafalgar. He is remembered with one of the world's most famous statues, Nelson's Column, in London's Trafalgar Square (of course).

The stories from the French trader and Admiral Villeneuve about the Revolution were true. It was a time so bloody and awful it was known simply as 'The Terror'.

Mad Mac, Lieutenant Darke and the crew of *Alerte* are fiction ... but the tales Mac tells of pirates are mostly true.

Pirates really were dirty, cruel and greedy. But their plunder was usually common cloth and spices, tea and sugar, not chests of glittering Spanish gold.

And the pirate of old?

Now he's gone and is at rest.

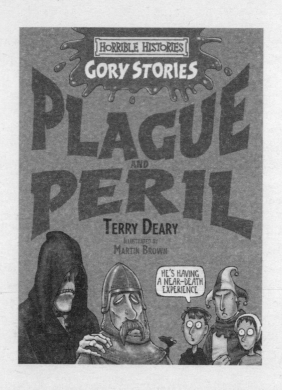

It's 1348 and the shadow of the Black Death is descending over England. Geoffrey Copton returns from the war in France, only to find himself caught up in a plot to rob and kill an innocent man. Will Geoffrey and his friend Meg manage to save the day, or will the dastardly plotters get away with the gold ... and with murder?

Find out in this Measly Middle Ages adventure, it's got all the gore and so much more!

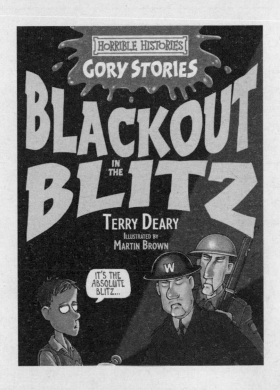

It's 1940 and Coventry is being targeted by German bombers. Alf and Sally are evacuated to Wales, but when Sally finds herself in the hands of the petrifying Mrs Pritchard, Alf plans an exciting escape. Will Sally be prepared for a flight in the moonlight?

Find out in this Woeful Second World War adventure, it's got all the gore and so much more!

Terry **Deary** was born at a very early age, so long ago he can't remember. But his mother, who was there at the time, says he was born in Sunderland, north-east England, in 1946 – so it's not true that he writes all *Horrible Histories* from memory. At school he was a horrible child only interested in playing football and giving teachers a hard time. His history lessons were so boring and so badly taught, that he learned to loathe the subject. *Horrible Histories* is his revenge.

Martin **Brown** was born in Melbourne, on the proper side of the world. Ever since he can remember he's been drawing. His dad used to bring back huge sheets of paper from work and Martin would fill them with doodles and little figures. Then, quite suddenly, with food and water, he grew up, moved to the UK and found work doing what he's always wanted to do: drawing doodles and little figures.